Promising

Jane Bailey

HEADLINE
REVIEW

First published in 1996
by HEADLINE BOOK PUBLISHING

First published in paperback in 1996
by HEADLINE BOOK PUBLISHING

A HEADLINE REVIEW paperback

10 9 8 7 6 5 4 3 2 1

ISBN 0 7472 5330 7

Printed and bound in Great Britain by
Cox & Wyman Ltd, Reading, Berks

HEADLINE BOOK PUBLISHING
A division of Hodder Headline PLC
338 Euston Road
London NW1 3BH

For Owen and Anna

Promising

Before each vacation, he and Willy Page discussed the possibilities. They talked about girls in a secret code, not one to ten like everyone else. Theirs was much more secret. There were Gateways who were OK, Harrods who were classy but after your money, Marks and Spencers who were not cheap but good quality, but the real scorers were Sainsburys. Neither of them had ever come close to a Sainsbury. At the beginning of each term they would greet each other, 'Any Sainsburys, then?'; 'No, she turned out to be a Safeway.' It was a disappointment, but there was a certain relief that the other had not got there first.

He lay back on the bed in his cramped boarding-school study, listening to the noise of the rain and pulling at newly sprouted hairs on his belly. The waiting was so long, like waiting for summer. But the only girls here were in the sixth form. Christ, something had to happen before he became one of that sad crowd.

When he wasn't loathing them for patronising him, Kieron felt sorry for the sixth-formers. Even when disobeying it, they respected the school hierarchy unquestioningly. Lower down the school they were all fighting for change, protesting at the brutally unfair subjection of younger boys to humiliating tasks. By the time they reached the sixth form they found they all had lucid arguments for accepting it whole-heartedly. So nothing ever changed. Winning ridiculous caps with silk tassels hanging from them for rowing or games mattered to them, and they wore them with pride for school photographs without feeling at all moronic. The girls all had Italianate names ending in 'a', and the boys swept their hair back a lot saying, 'Incredible'. In the winter they would go skiing in Switzerland, and in the summer they went on holiday to obscure places and bumped into each other. In the evenings they played with each other's computers or went out to smart restaurants with Francesca, Victoria, Amelia, Emma, Gemma, Fiona, Antonia, Olympia, Gabriella or Camilla. Incredible.

1

The cassette was ending for the third time. He looked down at his body, waiting for it to grow, waiting to be something, not a lean boy-man. Miles Frayling was already nearly six feet tall and he was five months younger than Kieron. He had thick muscles too and shoulders that girls swooned into. Probably. He said he had them queuing up when he visited the family home in St Tropez. But Kieron knew that Miles lived in Mudworth with his mother and the Royal Navy paid his fees.

He put the cassette on again and applied some lipsalve. Looking forward there was nothing but the drab predictability of school, but knowing that something had to start *soon* gave him a curious feeling of unease and excitement. He had grown bored with school. Mr Culpin had been the only really interesting teacher. He had worn unironed shirts in a selection of primary colours, and could change his voice to be anyone you wanted. But he had disappeared mysteriously at the end of last term (there were all sorts of rumours about why) and been replaced by Miss Swanbrook. Though there was some promise there, Willy reckoned.

Everything was promising. The bloody rain was promising. He ached for the summer. Something was going to happen this summer. It had to. Otherwise you could turn out to be one of those poor sods to whom it didn't happen until the age of seventeen or eighteen or – heaven forbid – after leaving school. And it wasn't just girls, there was something else. A yearning to be someone. Kieron often imagined saving a toddler from the wheels of a passing lorry; giving mouth-to-mouth resuscitation to one of the sixth-form (girls) knocked out on the hockey pitch; rescuing a suicide attempt by risking life and limb on the cliff by the bridge. 'YOUNG MAN SAVES LIFE IN HORROR ORDEAL!' No, it would be 'BOY'. Or would it? Perhaps it would be 'YOUTH'. He hated being this nowhere age. You couldn't even be a respectable hero.

He eyed his open suitcase which was still packed. There was his sticker book on the top. He had stopped collecting them two years ago, and wondered why he had taken it everywhere since the age of five. ('My smile's been to the dentist', 'Bear Necessities'). Now he collected words instead. He didn't write them in a book; he threaded them on strings inside his head and took them out to savour one by one. His latest was 'cleavage'. He rolled it around on his tongue, he sucked on it. It was a word of solid flavour. It heaved. It ravaged. It cleaved. Cleavage. He parted his lips and out it came.

2

'Cleavage!' He tilted his head back. 'Cleavage, cleavage, cleavage!'

Then he put it away to join languid, sensuous and mammary gland.

He lay on the bed, staring at an old deep crack in the corner of the ceiling, listening to the same song over and over. Please let it be a Sainsburys summer.

Ecstasy

This Friday was not an especially good day for Eve Swanbrook. She had hay fever. Her new work environment was alien. Her neighbour was hostile. She was thirty-two. Adrian, who had written two eminent books on Third World poverty, had not written her a birthday card. She was late for the doctor's.

As she was driving past the zoo she bumped into an elephant. Fortunately it did not seem hurt. The deeply creviced dun-grey skin had slightly flinched, and the bumper of Eve's car was mutilated.

'Sorry!' said the zoo assistant helpfully. 'I'm just taking Linda for a walk.'

'Why?'

'She's depressed.'

'Me too.'

Linda turned her sad grey head and looked at Eve sympathetically.

'Sorry!' said the zoo assistant again. 'You'll have to contact the zoo. I'm new.'

Eve looked out of the window to see the splinters of yellow sidelight on the road. It was a small price to pay for elephant empathy. She watched the animal's huge, loose-skinned, tiny-tailed bottom lumber apologetically on to the pavement and wondered if elephant valium would help her.

On the car seat beside her sat a lump of tree bark, a melon and a human skull called Colin which she needed for the Art class in an hour's time. She sped round the corner, already late for her appointment, only to find a long queue of traffic. A policeman, who looked like Frank Sinatra, was walking down the row of cars taking notes. He asked her to roll down the window.

'Why?' (Was he depressed too?)

'I'm afraid you're involved too, however slightly.'

'What in?'

4

'This pile-up.'

'I haven't been in a pile-up.'

He pointed to the front of her car. 'What's this, then?'

'Oh, that,' (relief), 'I just bumped into a depressed elephant.'

Frank smiled. Then he rummaged in his clothing (provocatively, she thought), and asked her to blow into a bag. She agreed miserably and wondered what it would be like to Do It His Way.

She arrived at the doctor's forty minutes late, carrying the skull, which was too valuable to leave in the car, and singing 'When I fall in love' unconvincingly to herself. The receptionist, who had lipstick on her teeth, was on the phone.

'I can fit you in on Tuesday at ten o'clock,' she said. (The people in the waiting room flicked through magazines quietly or were contemplating their illnesses.) 'I see, well, if it's urgent ... what is it exactly? ... Well, I can't make it urgent unless I know ... inflamed? ... suspected gonorrhoea ... you could try the clinic ... I see ... and your name? ... Greenway. Mrs? Miss ... Address?' (The people in the waiting room stopped flicking the pages of magazines and pondering their illnesses and started to ponder the lady on the phone, in case they had slept with her recently.) Then the receptionist repeated it all in case anyone hadn't heard.

'Can I help you?'

Colin's jaw dropped open, and Eve closed it. She wanted to give a false name but considered that news of her hay fever was unlikely to spread very far. She wondered fleetingly if she could suffocate the receptionist without anyone noticing, perhaps choke her with a wad of temporary address forms. But she didn't.

E.C.S.S. Willy studied the initials on the inside corner of Kieron's new exercise book, trying to pronounce them.

'Ecss ... You see, this is clearly a sign.'

'It's her initials,' said Kieron dryly. 'Give it a rest now, Willy. I'm trying to work.'

'That's your trouble. You'll never get anywhere if you ignore potent signs like this. If you take off the "s" and add "tasy" you've got "ecstasy"!'

Kieron looked up with tired disgust and applied some lipsalve: 'If you take off the "ecs" and add "tupid" you've got "stupid". So what do you think it means, Willy?'

Willy was digging fluff from his toenails with a compass end.

'Ecstasy,' he said. 'Oh, Ecstasy!'

And thus began the Miss Swanbrook fantasy. Willy reckoned

that she was in her prime and that women in their prime just craved boys their age. Kieron couldn't imagine Miss Swanbrook craving Willy Page, but he sucked the end of his pen and looked thoughtfully at his desk calendar. Willy had scampered off for proof, and returned with a limp, well-thumbed magazine. He thrust it at Kieron, grabbing his red Biro and underlining jaggedly two lines of print: 'Women therefore reach their sexual prime at about thirty or even later, whereas with men this tends to be considerably younger, around seventeen.'

'Well you've got another couple of years to wait, then,' Kieron had said, pretending lack of interest.

'One year one month, kiddo,' said Willy, snatching the magazine away. 'Anyway, it's all downhill after that. I'm just building up to it. I'll have her by the end of term, you wait.'

Kieron had laughed then, but when Willy had gone, he felt a curious protectiveness towards her. She wasn't a pin-up girl.

At thirteen he'd cut out a picture of a girl in a Tampax advert. She had thick dark eyebrows and a suggestive half-smile. He was completely bowled over. It had made him wild to think she was sharing the secret of her menstruation with him. It had made him quiver to think that a quarter of the women in the world were wearing tampons – there, up there, in that secret place – even as they were going about their everyday life. He still had the picture of the Tampax girl above his desk, but he wouldn't say who she was, not even to Willy. Now he thought he might take it down.

Anyway, he knew loads of women who disproved Willy's thesis. His Aunty Moira for a start. Moira kept a home for sick animals and wrote articles about them in the local paper back home. She made tea with lemon in it and wore socks under her skirts and her house smelt of dog. There was no way she was holding in rampant sexuality – though, come to think of it, she had taken in some student lodgers recently. No, they were at least eighteen. But it had said it there in print, so it must be true and Willy was right. And if Willy was right he didn't want him getting there first. He was pushy like that, Willy. You could just see him wheedling his way into women's affections with his small-talk. *If* Miss Swanbrook was sexually frustrated, just if, then it might just be bearable to help her out a bit. Not an ideal Sainsbury, really. But then she'd be experienced, and she'd take you to places and pay for you, like expensive restaurants, pop concerts and Europe, and no one would know, and you'd sit in classes and she'd give you back your book with a wink that no one else would see (except maybe

Willy and he'd be intrigued and jealous), and at the bottom of your work would be a cryptic comment like 'Good Work' or 'You're improving' and a secret sign and no one else would know not even the masters and she'd look all flushed and happy and give you 'A's for everything and write reports like: 'Kieron is very promising indeed.'

Oh, how ridiculous. Kieron closed his eyes and dreamt of Ecstasy.

Monday Morning

The alarm went off at 7.30 and Eve Swanbrook slammed her fist on the button. For once she hadn't dreamt of the sea. She feared the sea, and waves like child-snatchers that curled around your waist and dragged you down. After the initial irritation of the alarm, she was aware of having been transported from a warm and powerful atmosphere. She rolled on her side to recapture the image, but it had already slipped away. A cheek, an ear, a warmth. The alarm sounded again and she threw it on the floor.

Someone in the basement flat banged righteously on the ceiling with a broom handle. Eve Swanbrook made so little noise that she was convinced old Miss Crook did nothing but watch her go to work, watch her come home, and lie in wait for noise with broom in hand.

She spent five minutes trying to get her hay-fever drops to work, so that her eyes were red and swollen and she sniffled over breakfast. She went into the hall to collect the post and caught Nancy Crook reading everyone's postcards in the hallway. The neighbour pursed her grey moustached mouth and rocked heavily down the stairs with the limp she always assumed when trying to deflect attention from her misdemeanours.

Eve went back to her coffee with no post. She tore a piece of lined paper from a pad and wrote:

Dear Eve, (is it OK if I call you that now?)
You were wonderful last night. I don't think I'm too young, really I don't, but I won't tell anyone at school.
Your lover
XXX
PS. Do you really think it's illegal?

She put the note in an unsealed envelope addressed 'Miss Swanbrook – BY HAND – *PRIVATE*' and dropped it on the front mat as she went out.

Promising

* * *

In chapel assembly Eve tried to fit a familiar face to the presence in her dream. She searched through faces in her past and yearned to find this one.

> 'Breathe through the heats of our desire
> Thy coolness and Thy balm...'

they sang, and the eye irritation came back and made her nose and eyes stream. She rummaged vainly for a Kleenex and stood sniffing helplessly.

> 'Let sense be dumb, let flesh retire;
> Speak through the earthquake, wind and fire,
> Oh still small voice of calm
> Oh still small voice of calm.'

They all sat with a rustle, and the college chaplain, the Reverend Mr Hugo Cox, read the lesson. He was a wide ponderous man in his late forties, with a wide ponderous walk which made him look as though he were walking either side of a low barbed-wire fence anxious to avoid being grazed. He had a curious way of conversing which would confuse anyone, but as the Headmaster was the only person in the school to address Mr Cox, he was the only person confused by him.

'Good morning, Hugo,' the head would say.

'Thank you.'

'How are you?'

'Hello.'

'How's Mrs Cox keeping?'

'I'm fine, thank you. And yourself?'

'Oh, I'm very well, thank you. All set for Sunday chapel?'

'A bit iffy with her kidneys, but bearing up, Headmaster, bearing up.'

Hugo Cox spent most of his time studying the racing sections of the common-room newspapers, and had worked out an elaborate system of horse-winning possibilities for flat races, hurdles and chases on his home computer – so named because he had it at home, but which he had in fact borrowed permanently from the Science school, who had a new one now on insurance because they had reported a theft – breaking off occasionally

9

to give chapel services and the odd religious studies lesson.

His morning chapel services were brief and to the point. He had none of this modern shilly-shallying that went on in comprehensive schools. It wasn't that he was against it, but he left all that sort of thing to his young assistant chaplain who was fond of *involvement*, and would always involve at least half a dozen unwilling pupils in self-styled updates of biblical tales (where Jesus said lots of things like 'Hi' and 'Wow' and 'No way, Satan') and which were accompanied by a clattering self-orchestrated sing-song. These usually left the masters in a state of embarrassed shock, and the rest of the school in a state of apathetic bewilderment.

The Reverend Mr Cox preferred the cut and thrust of a good clean hymn, lesson, prayer, exit. He had been known to get them in the wrong order, or to say a totally inappropriate prayer, but he considered that improvisation was one of the perks of being experienced and he was quite happy to ad-lib.

'Dear God ... our Father ... Dear God our Father in Heaven ... look down on us at Downleaze College, and ... make us better people. When we are hungry, feed us. When we are ... ungrateful, make us grateful ... When we are ... bad, make us ... good. And bless all those who have examinations today ... or in the near future. Help them to do well ... or as well as they deserve. And may the First Fifteen win against Cheltenham on Saturday. For Christ's sake. Amen.'

He had not always been thus, but he believed that all men of the cloth underwent inevitable changes of heart and commitment throughout their careers. As a very young Hugo he had been startlingly committed. He had had a feverish sense of righteousness and an afflated desire to rid the world of injustice. As a child he had been inspired by the tale of the loaves and the fishes, and he could still remember how he had almost performed the miracle himself at the age of six, had his mother not stopped him angrily for ruining a good packet of Hovis thin-sliced and making the living room smell of fish. Oh, but all such energies wane, and Hugo Cox was going through a waning period during which time, he figured, it would be just as well to spend time profitably on the horses until things waxed again, although he wasn't terribly worried if they didn't.

Dark Secrets

'Can I move now?' asked Elvis.

'Ten more minutes, that's all,' Miss Swanbrook looked at the clock. 'Can you hold on that long?'

The fifth form were doing life-drawing today, and the model was a boy from the third form who was off games. Elvis was always off games, because he'd learnt where Matron's sick cards were and made up his own notes. He was especially good at 'migraine' since he'd learnt how to spell it, though he'd been caught out with 'head-ach' once.

Miss Swanbrook had asked him to look sporting for this pose, and he sat there surrounded by easels, sporting a pair of luminous Bermudas. His little knees stuck out jaggedly, and his white chest got smaller towards the armpits and showed all his ribs.

Eve was worried about his migraine. It seemed cruel to make him sit when he was in pain. But Elvis assured her he was fine so long as he wasn't playing rugger. Everyone knew he hated rugby because he was so small and weak. Once, in the scrum, he'd curled up so small with fear they'd mistaken him for the ball and booted him out. He'd broken two ribs and his nose, and had had migraine notes ever since.

But now Elvis was in his element. Surrounded by an audience, he could talk and know that everyone was listening. He was telling them all how he'd got A-minus for his painting of a cauliflower and how it would almost certainly be in the art exhibition.

'That's crap,' said Willy Page. 'I heard everyone else got A except you. You were the worst. The teacher just felt sorry for you.'

Elvis looked at his toes. Eve felt uncomfortable, making a mental note to give Elvis an A next time, no matter what. She was walking round the easels, looking over shoulders at images of muscly torsos. Whoever modelled, the pictures always looked like Popeye. Only Oakey had come close to the frail ribs of Elvis, and she stood

11

still and squinted at it. She took his pencil and measured an angle at the elbow.

'You see,' she said, leaning forward across Kieron's shoulder, 'you need to look at the spaces as well as the form.' And she redrew an angle.

Elvis looked smug because his angles were being looked at. As she stood up, her arm brushed against Kieron's face. It was warm. She stepped back, startled.

Kieron was wrong to imagine that he alone had spotted her reaction in assembly. At 'Breathe through the heats of our desire', the entire fifth form had looked at Ecstasy's face. Willy had gone on about it disgustingly all morning and he was getting on Kieron's nerves.

'The fact is,' he said after Art, 'she put her arm around me today while I was drawing. Did she put her arm around you? No.'

'Bollocks,' said Willy, 'she brushed against you, kiddo. I was there.'

'She had to make it look like that. But actually she was restraining herself.'

Willy looked revolted.

'Anyway,' said Kieron, looking modestly at his nails, 'I know a way of getting her alone.'

'Like what?'

'Well I'm not going to tell *you*, am I?'

'That's cos you're making it up.' But Willy looked worried.

'Oh no I'm not. In fact, I've been alone with her twice now. I'll tell you if things progress.'

Willy skulked off, saying he had better things to talk about. Real girls. But Kieron was worried in case he had given too much away. If Willy cottoned on to his method, that would be the end of it. And something else was bothering him too. It had just started to seem wrong talking about Ecstasy like this, especially since this morning. Something had made her more than Ecstasy or Miss Swanbrook today: a woman with dark secrets, a past, a present hidden to him. She wasn't like the girl on holiday who laughed at his thin legs. She wasn't like his sisters who pinched him slyly to make him confess things he hadn't done. She wasn't a woman like his mother who wore camel coats. She was a woman with tags hanging out of her clothes and the prices on the soles of her shoes. She was a woman with eyes like the sea. She was a woman with something on her mind. Something in chapel had made Miss Swanbrook cry.

Saturday Night Detention

'Why do you keep doing this?' She handed him two more sheets of A4.

'Dunno.' He stuck his chewing-gum on the corner of the desk, avoiding her eyes. He realised he had forgotten his lipsalve and felt suddenly naked. His lips weren't at all dry, but the thought that they might become dry made them feel like paper. He was uneasy.

It was 8.45 p.m. A drainpipe dripped heavily on to the window-ledge. Kieron Oakey looked thoughtful and swallowed, setting a lump stirring under the skin of his throat. He pushed up his sleeves. Then his head was down and he was writing fast. He had parted his hair in various places so that a jagged white path made its way over his dark head. A pink spot glistened next to an ink spot at the corner of his long nose, until his head bent further. Miss Swanbrook stared bleakly at the lean neck, the bone sticking up whitely. A large tag flapped outside his jumper:

'Hand wash at 40° C. Dry flat. Cool iron,' and then in large red letters: 'DO NOT WRING'. It seemed to be a warning against her vengeful designs on his neck.

She looked away and picked at tufts of wool on her cardigan as she re-read Oakey's unacceptable first attempt:

'What this school has given me,' it was entitled. 'This school has given me lots of things. Loads of detentions, headaches, C-minuses and glandular fever. It has also given me lots of nice teachers. My Art teacher is called Miss Swanbrook although nobody knows why she isn't Mrs because there are millions of superb masters like Avery for example or Felix or Mr Biddle no he's married but he wouldn't mind. Mr Avery is a big strong Gym teacher with everything a woman could want I should think, though I suppose he is a bit spotty. Felix may be a bit old for Miss Swanbrook but he has quite a big house near Bath though he probably prefers men. Perhaps Miss Swanbrook prefers women . . . but I digress. This school has given me a *brilliant* education and I

13

don't deserve it. I am a lazy, good-for-nothing slacker and I should know better. At my age. What would my parents think if I behaved like this at home?

'Now I shall have to stop unfortunately as unfortunately my pen is running out – come back you little bastard!!! ... probably gone for a leak...' (a large blue blot covered the remainder of the page) '...obviously couldn't wait.' Then, in enormous letters to cover the whole of the second side:

'I AM SO GRATEFUL TO EVERYONE HERE. THE SKY IS GREY. THERE IS A PIGEON ON THE WINDOWSILL. MISS SWANBROOK IS WEARING A BLUE SKIRT.'

She looked up to see his long white grateful fingers writing earnestly, the down dark on his warm arms. The windows were steaming up and she could smell the damp wool of his pullover. A money-spider was climbing a ladder up it from elbow to shoulder. It was ten to nine. It negotiated a rickety journey through some hairs at the nape of his neck and disappeared into his hairline. He scratched, and she noticed for the first time the gleaming satin curves inside his ears. The rain dripped faster and faster on to the ledge. Oh God. Another Saturday night. She had only volunteered for Saturday night detention duty because everyone knew it was never used. But this was the second Saturday two weeks into term.

Kieron Oakey had been almost good enough to go up a set at the beginning of term, and she had had high hopes that he might. Now she wondered if he would deteriorate fast enough to go down a set, but she seemed stuck with him. She moved over to the window and rubbed a patch in the wet glass. Down in the quadrangle a drenched magnolia tree displayed tall thick blooms and buds like candles waiting to be lit.

At last he flung down his pen with a sigh and handed her the second attempt. He waited while she finished reading it.

'I won't be put down, will I, Miss?'

'Don't worry.' She attempted a steely glare. 'I know a good vet who can do it quite painlessly.'

He smiled, reassured, and left the door open behind him. She gathered up bits of paper from under his desk and tried to remove the chewing gum. It was 9.15. The pink goo wouldn't come off, and bits of it stuck under her nails.

Friends in Need

Eve's Monday night boarding duty was slow to end, and she closed her diary miserably after surveying her weekend. There wasn't much free time. On Friday evening she was covering for someone else's duty and on Saturday night it might be detention again. On Sunday there was chapel. If Adrian rang she wouldn't be there.

'Let's go nude!'

'What?'

Felix, a middle-aged master with long whiskers, was already throwing off his tie. Avery started to unbutton his shirt, 'Great idea!'

'You're not serious, are you?' Eve Swanbrook yawned. Boarding duty had just finished and she had accepted a drink at the house tutor's flat. But now she was tired, and she wanted to go home.

'Come on, Eve. Get your clothes off, sweetheart!'

'Not a chance!' She glanced nervously at Felix who was already down to some rather off-white Y-fronts.

'Don't be such a prude!'

Were they joking? She looked for her handbag, just in case, and crossed her cardigan in front.

'Honestly, I was just off. It's gone eleven. I've loads to do tomorrow. No really, I must be going.'

'I'm surprised at you, Eve.' Rob Avery, the twenty-five-year-old hunk of Kieron's essay was unbuckling his trouser belt, 'I thought you were a good laugh.'

'Well I'm not. I'm boring. And I'm going.'

'God, Eve. Just take your top off.'

Felix was putting a record on the tiny stereo in the corner. The room was shadowy. He'd hung a sock over the lamp. Most of the light came from a frosted window into the passage and two electric rings which he'd lit on the stove to keep the tutor's flat warm.

15

Eve didn't want bad relations with her new colleagues, but she was very tired. She just wanted to go home.

'You're both drunk,' she said decisively, and got up to go. Rob Avery pushed her back on the stained sofa and sent a mug of wine over a pile of coursework on the floor. 'Shit! Now look what you've made me do!'

Eve bent to clear it up. She held up a sheet of paper and the red liquor dripped down it on to the carpet, as the careful blue writing turned into violet streams.

'Oh, never mind,' said Rob, shaking the last drop from the mug over the papers, 'there's more wine in the bottle. Come on, have a drink.'

'I've had one.'

'Have another.'

'I'm tired.'

'The night is yet young!'

'Look, I'm going.'

'You boring old fart.'

'Look, I find this a bit ... threatening.'

'*Threatening*? You don't think——?' Felix laughed, but he wasn't quite sure of his ground.

'Honestly, Eve,' said Avery, 'you're so naïve. We're your *friends*. For Christ's sake...' He was pouring a can of beer into a glass measuring jug. 'I think you need a drink. Come on, just one drink. Then we'll let you go.'

'If you take your top off,' added Felix.

'Good-bye, Ruby Tuesday...' croaked the record. 'Who could hang a name on you...?'

Eve bit the edge of her mouth and accepted a mug of wine. After all, they were the only friends she had here. There was a lull while Avery made toast, Eve's handbag over his naked shoulder. She planned to drink quickly and to go while they were busy munching.

The wine tasted of gin, and a chip in the glass caught her lip as she drank. She could see Felix sitting cross-legged in dark red socks. He was singing along to the music with his eyes closed. Two distorted nipples looked sadly from the face of his bent chest, his navel like the hole of a small burrowing animal in a bank of undergrowth.

The sight of this strange Buddha set her laughing, shooting wine back into the mug. It calmed her nerves and she decided to drink some more and laugh the whole thing off. Encouraged by wine and opportunity, Felix started to tickle her, and Rob Avery came over from his toasting to jump on her.

Moments later she was topless, face down, under the full weight of Felix who sat astride her semi-naked, massaging her back with cooking oil. Kieron had been wrong about him.

'Just a quick massage before you go home. It'll help you to sleep better.'

Things were swimming before her. She was aware of them discussing women, young women – girls. Familiar names. They were laughing. She could see Rob Avery sitting on the sofa, naked but for a pair of red and white striped boxer shorts on his head, giving him a curiously biblical look. She looked at his crossed feet inches from her nose. Great yellow soles with damp gangly toes clamped the sodden exam papers to the floor. 'Dentists do it in your mouth', read the empty mug on the carpet and, about a yard away, she could see the green noose of Felix's discarded tie.

'My go,' said Rob and, as Felix got up, Eve scrambled to her feet, clutching her clothes to her chest.

'I must go to the loo.'

With the door locked, she sat on the toilet seat and breathed out deeply. She must keep calm. Stuck on to the tiles with Blu-tack was a surfing postcard, and she shuddered. It was a long way from the sea. But they had claws like waves that would pull her down. She looked around her. There was no window. An extractor fan purred above her, and over the bath three or four more pairs of off-white or off-blue Y-fronts dripped loudly from a line.

Her eyes scanned vaguely for something to read within distance of the toilet. Reading always helped Miss Swanbrook to relax. To one side was a fluoride toothpaste tube. On the floor were some empty toilet rolls and a curious, long slender carton. She picked it up:

'Remington Hygienic Clipper. Safe personal trimmer for nose, ear and eyebrow hair. Easy to clean. Uses LR6 batteries. Our price, £9.95.'

She was stirred into action. She went to the door and listened. There were no voices coming from the lounge, only the record player panting, 'Let's spend the night together.' She opened the door quietly and tiptoed into the passage.

She ran down the back corridor of the boarding house, the blouse sticking to her oily back. She ran out into the night, past the boys smoking by the bins, past her own parked car, past the dark whispering park, until she was home. She spent the night shivering on the doorstep. Her handbag was on Avery's shoulder.

Façade

'You coming to lunch?' Felix emerged from behind the pigeon-holes where he had been lying in wait.

'Yes, I'm just coming.'

He accompanied his lady colleague over to the refectory. 'What are you doing on Friday?'

'Boarding duty.'

'Poor you. What about Saturday?'

'Well...' Eve couldn't think of anything in particular.

'I'm thinking of getting some tickets to the theatre: *One Flew Over the Cuckoo's Nest*. Fancy coming?'

Going to visit relatives? Marking? Already something planned? No – hesitation, too late for that one. Detention duty? No one in it yet.

'Well ... can I think about it?'

'Sure,' Felix purred, opening the refectory door for her with his fat paw. 'It's got good reviews. You'd love it.'

They queued behind the pupils, and Eve felt a shudder when she thought she saw a group of boys smirking in front of them. She tried to dissociate herself from Felix, but he kept laying claim to her. He pushed back some boys roughly, 'Make way for a lady, will you?' and, turning to her: 'No manners these boys.' Kieron Oakey looked round at her reproachfully.

At the staff table two rows of grey men sat talking, showing only their bottom teeth. It was as though their top lips had been permanently clamped to their top teeth by some vengeful orthodontist bent on turning them all into newscasters. Small wonder they had difficulty eating the spaghetti. They were discussing cricket very aggressively. Eve listened, bemused, as tempers rose over the toings and froings of a small leather ball, and watched as the little orange streaks of spaghetti slopped more frequently across more florid faces. As one master slammed off in a cricket tantrum to get some water, she attempted a change of conversation.

19

'Why did Mr Culpin leave?'

There was a silence. Just the clinking of cutlery.

'The man I replaced?' she ventured.

Glances were being exchanged. 'We don't talk about that,' said Someone Senior at the head of the table. 'Touch sensitive. Hush-hush and all that.'

Eve searched Felix's face for an answer.

'The *official* reason: he fucked little boys.' He slurped loudly on his spaghetti. 'Basically.'

A murmur went round the table. Someone may have disagreed.

'And Avery here fucks little girls,' he added to break the tension. Everyone chortled.

Felix was pleased that, despite being a woman, Eve had managed to fit in so well with the jocular crowd at the table. He was pleased that it was he who had brought her over to lunch, and he was pleased too that he was making headway with her on the romantic front.

Felix Lamb was a lofty, loose-fleshed man of fifty-four. He had been an only child, the pride and joy of his mother who, having scolded him constantly for not pronouncing his words properly, had left him with the legacy of a slight speech defect concerning his esses which made him sound like a salivating voice-over advertising fruit pies. He had been the first amongst his school friends to reach puberty which, in mixed surroundings, might have stoked in him a brazen manfulness, but in a single-sex environment had left him merely abashed and bewildered, with a deep throaty croak which emphasised his sibilant defect, and a slight stoop. It was during adolescence that he had fallen in love with food. Away from home and affection, he had put everything remotely edible or suckable into his mouth as consolation, and had developed a hard, tumescent belly which grew limper now with age. He had often fancied himself pregnant, and had recurrent dreams that he was. He had always wanted children and had never imagined that he wouldn't, at the age of fifty-four, have two or three bright young offspring calling him Dad and keeping him on his toes with the latest trends. Unable to have a baby of his own, and overwhelmed by a desire to produce, Felix Lamb had written prodigiously for the past ten years. His first book, *One Hundred Years of Downleaze College*, had been rejected by seventeen publishers for a variety of reasons ('unfortunately unlikely to be of interest to a wide readership', 'lacking in spice', 'drab and pompous in style') and his second book, *A Traveller's Guide to Africa*, had received only two rejections so far. This was not a major problem, he considered: the prospective publishers had rejected it on the grounds of having 'terribly', 'awfully' and 'jolly' sprinkled far too liberally in the text, along with generous clusters of 'incredible', 'amazing', 'tremendous', 'uncivilised' and 'primitive', with combinations such as 'jolly uncivilised', 'awfully amazing' and 'incredibly primitive' arousing special censure. Felix brimmed with modest pleasure at the simplicity of the solution. He instantly rewrote his tome, omitting all the jolly awfully terribly incredible amazing tremendous uncivilised primitive words, and sent it off again, although he already suspected that something was wrong before the publishers wrote back six months later explaining that this had reduced it to a large pamphlet.

Despite his lack of success in the literary field, Felix Lamb had a spacious house, a thick ginger moustache and a way with women. He didn't meet many women, but when he did, he had a way with them. His way was to bulldoze through all their rejections and badger them into his company. He knew a lot about women. He knew they liked persistent men, trips to the theatre and candlelit dinners, and above all he knew (from Cary Grant and James Bond) that when they said 'no' they really meant 'yes'.

Visiting her pigeon-hole before going home, Eve Swanbrook found two orange card tickets for the theatre on Saturday night. A little note said: 'Had to buy them – they were the last two. See you Saturday, 7.30 – F.'

She resolved to put some poor child in detention for absolutely anything.

She had known orange card like this before. When she was five she was in Orange Group. She had loved the pictures they were shown each day: the dappled green Apple, the purple Box, the Car with the headlight eyes. And then one day they were asked to say the words. Each child stood up in turn and chanted until they faltered somewhere around P or Q. Eve had stood in blank panic. Why didn't anyone *tell* you you were supposed to be learning the letters? Why show you all those pictures, then? She could have drawn them all: the glorious Queen, the Sock with the Squirrel in it, the smiling Teapot, the Rabbit, the red-nosed Uncle. Why didn't anyone say? It was some kind of trick, all of it. And how come all the others were in on it too? There was Red Group, Blue Group,

Green Group and Orange Group. Orange Group had an orange card squirrel on the group of tables to console its retardees, none of whom were ever expected to get as far as Squirrel.

The outline of the college's founder sharpened against pale gold clouds gathering on the horizon. A heavy wind set the flag flapping at its pole, and Miss Swanbrook's skirt flattened against her thighs as she crossed the quadrangle at dusk. On one side the field, on the other three the dark mock-Gothic buildings standing crisply against the low-lit sky. The central campus, with its mullioned windows, elaborate trefoil and cinquefoil tracery and slender, panelled buttresses topped with gargoyles or pinnacles, rose immodestly beside the 'Pop-In' launderette and a day centre for the blind. On the other side the new computer block looked like a slab of vanilla icecream, and a modern designer construction perched incongruously on a roof by the chapel. She opened an oak door with flowing iron scrollwork and headed for home. She had felt uneasy all day and was relieved as she crossed under the huge foliated arch of the school façade, leaving behind her the great auricular mouldings to strain and listen.

Our Secret

Miss Swanbrook looked pleased to see Kieron again on Saturday night. In fact, the more he thought of it, the more he was convinced there was something between them. He'd tried really hard to get put in detention by Felix again this week, but hadn't succeeded. Then he'd tried skipping Mr Durrant's lessons and that hadn't worked either. Even being rude to the senior master only got him gated for the weekend. But Ecstasy had come to the rescue. She had slammed him in detention just for forgetting his exercise book. What about that, then? There was some real collusion here, and he knew it.

He gave her a warm lipsalved smile as he sat down. She smiled back, a mature woman's smile.

'I'm sorry I overreacted a bit,' she confided, 'but you have to learn.'

'That's OK, Miss,' he grinned knowingly. 'I quite like detentions.'

Her face changed. 'Oh. Well, you're not supposed to like them. What can I give you to do that you don't like?'

Take me in your arms. I'd hate that. Come and ravage me. Drop your blue skirt and bend over the desk. I couldn't stand it. Punish me any way you like.

'Um. Well, I don't like essays that much, actually.' Brush my face again. Tie me to the desk.

'Actually,' she said breezily, 'I don't much like marking them either. I'll tell you what, though. I'll let you go at 8.15 if you don't tell anybody.'

'Thanks.' Now what was she playing at? 'Our secret, Miss,' he winked.

Who was he? He once heard of a gypsy woman who sold her baby for a bag of plums. He thought he might be the son of a dark traveller, and not his parents' son. When they spoke to him they didn't reach him, and his words just seemed to roll off

23

their waxed surfaces. He had dark hair and feared wearing shorts because of his thin legs. He shouldn't be here, he knew that. He should be selling pegs and watching the sun rise over Stonehenge.

An eight-year-old neighbour called Jessica Brace once let him fly her kite and asked him: 'Look, do you love me or what?' and made him chase her through a field. She zipped him up in her parents' tent and hovered over him.

'I bet you can't guess what I'm thinking of doing! It begins in "k" and ends in "g".'

He trembled out 'kissing'. She squealed, 'Kiting!' and whirled off laughing with her spiteful ribbon-tailed kite.

There were so many people you couldn't understand, and who wouldn't understand you. And there was a loneliness in being with them.

Miss Swanbrook gave him a perky little title again: 'Why this term is so important', and he started writing.

This term was so important because this term you had exams. He looked up at the head bent over a book, the soft down around the ears and at the nape. And this summer was what decided your whole future. The clean nails and the slender fingers holding the page. And you might not get to university if you didn't get good grades. The pale throat disappearing into the neck of a pink blouse. And you could only get good grades if you worked hard. It was no good thinking you could just cruise along. Just because you were bright didn't mean you'd get good grades. The soft cardigan rolled up at the sleeves, the piece of hair falling over her eyes flicked back gently. She wasn't looking at him. You had to try really hard. You had to do your best. He could feel her looking at him. And you had to start early, not leave it all till the last minute. The soft perfume in the air, the pale stockings under the desk. This summer was really the most important summer of his whole life.

Very Important People

Fifty yards away, on the same Saturday evening the guests at the headmaster's dinner table were discussing the introduction of girls into the sixth-form over a first course of dark spare ribs.

'And another thing, what on earth do you call them?' said Mr Cuthburtson, the senior housemaster. 'I've been calling them by their surnames and they get most upset. But you can't call the damn things by their Christian names or the boys will want to be John and Darrell next, and then, God knows, we'll produce a bunch of pooftas.'

Mr Cuthburtson was shallowly religious and thought to be good for the moral spine of the school. He talked about God a lot, as though He were an ex-headmaster or an eminent old boy. He loathed women. Except his wife. He had to like her a little bit as she saw that his washing and cooking got done – by someone else – and slept with him. She even allowed him to indulge in his fantasies. She would spank him, whip him, and tie him to the bed with soft ropes he had attached to the corners for this purpose. He had never tied her up, although she would have liked it. Instead, she lay in bed dreaming of being seduced by the sixth-form boys in their house or coaxed into submission by millionaires from the old boy network.

'All the research shows that boys work better in a mixed environment,' said the blonde, petite woman quietly, 'and that, if anything, it's the girls who fare the worst.'

Mrs Cuthburtson was only the wife of Mr Cuthburtson, and her views were given a polite hearing. Mrs Cuthburtson knew this, watching with a look of admiring deference as her husband continued his views nasally, and she reflected how much she found him, as the years went by, to be more and more of a pompous fathead.

At one end of the table sat Mrs Montague. She was the headmaster's wife and very important indeed, though not as important as she felt she ought to be. She wanted calm before the main course to allow admiration of her cook's Jamaican chicken, and so changed the subject to fashion. She had designed the new girls' uniform and had designs on the chairman of the governors, Mr Craven. She sparkled across the table at him, 'What do you think of the girls' uniform, Jeremy?'

'Oh, very fetching indeed. Well, no, very ... smart, yes.' He caught his wife's eye. 'If it had been left to me I would have waited until the time was *right* for mixing. We weren't quite *ready* for girls, but the pressure was on us. It's what the parents are looking for these days. And I do think we've managed it more smoothly than most other public schools in our group.'

The chairman of the governors was exceptionally important. He sat at the head of the table with iron-grey hair and an iron-grey suit, enveloped in a general grey sockiness. He was considered by most to be distinguished, although he had little to distinguish him from anyone apart from three expensive cars, four expensive houses and an inexpensive wife called Iona.

He was one of three sons, had been to an all-boys prep school, an all-boys public school, and an all-male Oxford college. He had tried in vain to meet girls, but there were only the Radcliffe nurses who were too terrifyingly buoyant and womanly, or the crisp, angular students from the women's colleges who were bolted in at night and who were all far too sharp and articulate to be sensual prey to moderately articulate men such as Jeremy Lancelot Craven, who had only got in to read Classics after he'd been rejected for PPE and his father had kicked up a rumpus.

Iona had spotted him in St Aldate's church in her third year when time, as her mother had said, was running out. She knew it was essential to meet a steady, unremarkable man who could provide for her, and had snapped up Jeremy Lancelot by Ascension day. She had worn paper-thin woollen pullovers and allowed her skirt to ride up ever so slightly on the prayer cushion so that Jeremy, who knew nothing of women but only knew he wanted one, found it hard to resist. She told him she was all for sex, and that Christians should never be ashamed to enjoy it, but only after marriage. It was this last clause which wrapped it up for Iona, and she had him trembling at the altar before he fumbled his way through her reluctant maidenhead.

After the first few weeks of marriage their lovemaking became less and less frequent. Iona felt sex was altogether too messy a business to dwell on or explore. She would wince with irritation when she felt the stirrings in Jeremy's pyjamas, close her eyes, and remain completely immobile as he got on with the wretched process, until the soft tag of flesh flopped repentent in his pyjama bottoms.

Jeremy Lancelot Craven had had the idea, quite early on, of dealing with the problem entirely by himself, but the moment Iona sensed the soft brushings of self-abuse between the sheets, she would call him a disgusting animal, so that his mental picture of a blonde Amazon would be wrenched away along with his desire. He had resorted to relief in the bathroom, but Iona, suspicious of the time spent in there alone, had removed the bolt from the door on the pretext that it could be dangerous with young children about. She never hesitated to pop her rodent head around the door at some stage during his ablutions – particularly when there were no wash-like splashings – to check if the water was hot enough. After four years of marriage he had turned to prostitutes, but this too had been scuppered when Iona's sharp nose had sniffed a foreign odour on his Aertex vest. Ever since then she examined his underwear meticulously before putting it in the wash, and refused his offer to hire an au-pair to do the washing, like everyone else.

Iona had a skinny crop of hair that hung in meagre clumps on either side of her red ears. Her sensitive nose pointed up so sharply that you could hook a coat on it. Jeremy had stopped looking at her body, but he knew that her nipples felt cold and flat like two drawing pins in an empty board. The only thing Iona Craven possessed which was the envy of other women and their husbands was a wide, mobile, pouting mouth. Jeremy tried not to look at this as it had never fulfilled its promise. He had rarely been able to kiss it, and had never been able to do with it what he really wanted.

He hated his wife and had recurrent fantasies about killing her. These started seriously thirteen years ago when the deft six from his cricket bat landed with a smart 'thlock' on the side of his wife's head while she was sitting forward on a deckchair and sent her keeling face-down into a plate of avocado dip. He had been shocked by the uncomfortable feeling he'd had when the radiant doctor said it would be all right. He had gone home and been sick in the bath, and had been pushing her out of moving vehicles or nonchalantly leaving her in garbage-grinding lorries ever since.

Iona pursed her mouth. 'It's the knock-on effect that worries me,' she said, watching her husband in her peripheral vision. 'It's all very well having women staff in the masters' common room, but can they control the boys? I can't see it myself.'

Iona Craven loathed her husband because he had never given her any foreplay. From the very first she had felt excluded from their lovemaking and grown to resent feeling a mere tool for his pleasure. She listened to Mr Cuthburtson with admiration, nodding vigorously and wondering what it would be like to lie beneath him. She watched his long fingers playing with the wine glass and uncrossed her legs under the table.

The headmaster, Mr Montague, was baffled by the whole co-educational experiment, and not sure whether to be proud or distraught about adopting it in his school. 'I think...' He was slow to formulate sentences from his ideas and tried to wait until everyone was chewing in order to interject, but he failed except to ask if anyone wanted more wine.

Mrs Cuthburtson had said very little all evening and was now very flushed. She had watched the sharp pink tongue of the headmaster flick out and remove some thick juice near his lip.

The chairman of the governors was also being watched. He had never been aware of being sexually attractive to anyone before he met his wife, but since he had become filthy rich he found that women eyed him in the same promising way his wife had done in St Aldate's church. He did not make the connection himself, and assumed that the tragic lust in the eyes of the headmaster's wife was merely part of the same taunting game played by his wife thirty years previously. Nonetheless, evenings such as these offered the luxury of boltable bathrooms, so he rose after his spare ribs, cast a defiant glance at his wife, and excused himself.

Precocious Tarts

There had been nothing left to Saturday night when Eve returned home after detention. There wasn't even the luxury of a lie-in the following morning because of chapel. The alarm had already bleeped 8.30. Eve Swanbrook was having another go at the latest dream. She had been walking by water – a beach, perhaps, walking by the dunes with ... Kieron Oakey. Good heavens. And there was a sense of conspiracy. Something between them. They had been up to something together ... Gosh. And they'd bumped into Felix ... or was it Avery? Or was it the head himself? And Kieron had turned to her and said softly, 'Our secret', and *winked*. She replayed the wink scene repeatedly as she lay watching the curtains. The curious thing was, she could imagine Kieron doing just that in real life.

At 10 a.m. she was in the school chapel, her tiered pew facing the tiered pews of the fifth forms. She couldn't help searching for Kieron's face in the crowd, as if it might tell her something; after all, less than two hours ago they had been up to something together.

She was sure he was looking at her, and almost certain that Willy Page was nudging him. But each time she looked the great crow figures of black-gowned staff seemed to block the view. Felix seemed to take up two places because he stood with his feet apart and thrust his elbows out.

Eve had just walked down the aisle into the daylight when she felt Felix on her tail. With vast strides he overtook her.

'Guess what! I managed to change those tickets for tonight, so you'll be able to see it after all.'

Eve's smile froze on her face. She hadn't the heart or the energy to counter this one. And anyway, she was unconsciously looking for Kieron in the crowd of boys spilling out of chapel. And yes, he did turn round and look at her, and so did that boy with him. Willy Whatsit. And no wonder: Avery had his hand on her shoulder.

'Do come for a drink afterwards – we're all going down the Ship.'

'Now?'

'No, after your theatre trip with Felix. We'll be down the Ship after ten, OK?' and he was gone.

She stood for a moment in the sunshine, chatting to people politely. It couldn't go on like this. Surely something had to happen in life. This summer was going to be hot. The chapel windows stared blackly at her in the fierce light, and she couldn't help feeling that the headmaster was watching her. Why did Miss Swanbrook leave? Icy silence. But why did she go, the woman I replaced? We don't talk about that. That woman had to go. She dreamt about little boys, Felix would say, basically.

'Basically,' said Felix, 'it questions whether sane people live inside institutions or out.'

His stomach was spilling out over his trouser tops and he sat with his knees very wide in the theatre seat next to hers. He was very excited and had worked up quite a sweat. The pungent Felix odour seemed to fill the left half of the upper circle, and there was no escaping it.

The curtain went up again and the great Felix knee pressed into hers. Eve turned her knees away, trying at the same time to tilt her body in the same direction. But the arm came up and draped over the back of the seat. Great wafts of Felix came from the shamelessly exposed armpit, and now the entire upper circle needed oxygen. She leant so far in the opposite direction that she was pressing into her neighbour, a youngish gentleman sitting alone in Eau Sauvage. He seemed to return the pressure, and then his foot hooked around hers. She instantly thrust her knees back Felixward, and the huge paw came down on her shoulder.

Eve sat sandwiched for a while, then whispered to Felix that she was ill: she'd see him down at the Ship. She was glad that it was dark and that she wouldn't see the whiskers droop and the hurt in his face.

Eve spotted Avery straight away. He was sitting at a corner table on his own. He looked startled when he saw her.

'You're early ... have a seat.'

'I felt ill.'

'Have a drink.' He was getting up, but she insisted that she didn't feel like one yet, just to look convincing. But there was something odd about Avery this evening. He wore a faded red T-shirt and jeans and looked a lot younger and more casual than usual. And in his face she could detect an uneasiness at her presence. His eyes were shifting away from hers and he was itching to get up.

'Good God!' he said suddenly.

Eve turned around and saw a tall, beautifully dressed girl coming towards the table. She recognised her as a lower-sixth-former.

'What are you doing here?' he asked curtly. 'If you don't go now I shall have to report you.'

The girl looked very indignant and glared, tight-lipped, at Avery, then at Eve.

'Look,' he said nervously, taking the girl by the elbow and steering her towards the door, 'if you go now we shall say nothing of it.'

The girl left, turning to look once more at Eve as Avery shuffled her out.

'Precocious little tarts,' said Avery, returning to the table. 'They're underage – you've got to be firm with them.'

But Eve was staring at the second half-full glass where she was sitting, and the black cardigan on the stool next to hers.

Common Scents

The invigilation room was filled with the thick smell of sweat. The summer examinations were already starting in mid-May, and they allowed an opportunity for extensive staff day-dreaming. Eve moved wearily up and down the rows of desks handing out more paper, watching them. Kieron put up his hand to ask about a misprint, and as she neared him she breathed in his smell.

Eve had located three main man scents, along with a host of subgroups. There was Socky, which was common in classrooms, and generally smelt bitter. There was the unpleasant smell which some men had, like Felix. It smelt like the circuses she remembered from childhood where they had elephant enclosures. This smell she called Elephant. Fortunately, not many men were Elephant. Then there was Woody, a rather sweet, resiny, woody smell. Kieron Oakey, for example, was decidedly Woody.

The governors' meeting which took place at 6.15 p.m. was intended for the bringing together of staff and school governors in an Informal Context.

There was a crowd in the masters' common room. The first man Eve recognised was the deputy chairman of the governors. He looked like Lord Lucan. Then she recognised the pompous man from the lunch table the day before. He looked like Lord Lucan too. She felt conspicuous in a sea of grey men.

There were two types of grey men, she thought. The first wore grey. They were generally career men. They had perhaps two grey suits and always wore black shoes. They were well groomed and very occasionally smelt of aftershave or fabric conditioner. The second type usually wore polished horsechestnut shoes. These men wore mud-coloured jackets with dung-coloured trousers, clean each month, and were prevalent at Downleaze College. They carried mottled handkerchiefs and smelt of stale sweat. Classic Socky men.

Promising

The informal occasion continued arduously for over an hour. Eve stood loosely connected to a circle which included the headmaster and his wife.

The headmaster was a man in his late forties with slim hands and a slim nose that looked as if it had been ironed. He spoke preciously, as if every slightly nasal word cost him a supreme intellectual effort and might be very valuable some day. In fact he spoke slowly because he was a dim, pedestrian thinker. He needed to gather signs of his success around him. Behind his desk was a picture of himself at Oxford (Christ Church Freshmen 1968), and a large shiny oar strung up on the wall. He felt uncomfortable in large groups – especially ones which included his wife – and was not at all at ease now.

The headmaster's wife had married beneath her. She had been manageress of the swimwear department at Rackhams before she met Peter, and one of her suitors had been an earl. Well, the best friend of an earl. Anyway she could have married a millionaire shipping magnate – only she hadn't been ready. Heaven knows he'd asked her enough times. But now here she was: a handsome, tight-lipped woman without two villas to mention together.

Opposite stood the only other female teacher, Miss King, a chinless woman with sensible shoes. She always wore beige ('beige goes with everything') and brown ('brown goes so well with beige') giving her the look of an old British Rail platform pillar. She fantasised on weekends about her encounter in 1967 with an Oxford don who had fondled her breasts in the Botanical Gardens. She remembered the hard thighs pressing into hers and wondered what would have happened if she hadn't slapped him and said she was saving herself for the man she married. Oh, fateful vow! Now she would lie in bed on Saturday nights straddling him in her sleep, gripping the white academic biceps and breathing in the odour of his pale remembered neck.

Mr Solomon, head of Classics, left his favourite chair to brush shoulders with Eve and inspect her breasts. He had never married, and thought endlessly of his one near miss. Marian Allsop had walked out with him for an evening debate in Cambridge when her fiancé was ill. He would never forget the hard little buds under her pullover and the warmth of her soft skin. They filled his fantasies, and had left him with the desire to unbutton every blouse, to feel every bosom, every day of his life, for as long as he lived. Almost each day to be inches away from a whole selection of sixth-form-girls' breasts was an unbearable promise of paradise.

He would flutter around their bent heads and point to words in their exercise books with careful brushes against those warm mounds. Since the arrival of girls at Downleaze College his teaching objectives had changed. He longed for problems he could point to, he ached for imperfect work and spelling mistakes.

Eve wondered what she was doing here. When she was three she'd wanted to be a steamroller driver. She'd wanted to smooth out uneven surfaces, smell hot tar and eat jelly babies. Then she'd wanted to marry Teddy Bowan, run a fairground and sleep on a bed of candyfloss. She had wanted to paint animals, and then she had wanted to paint people. She had never wanted to feel loneliness in crowds.

She eventually found refuge in the Reverend Mr Hope, the ageing former chaplain of the college. Mr Hope should have left years before but had been allowed to stay on because he refused to leave the small garden flat which went with the post, and he was good at selecting winners on the horse-racing. He was very partial to his garden which housed a huge selection of gnomes who would be homeless if he left. Eve, whose flat overlooked his, had often seen him talking to his gnomes in the early mornings. Now he was telling her of his great passion which had led to his vast collection of Deanna Durbin cuttings. He had sent the star lots of letters when he was younger and had seen her passing in a taxi in 1962. He still corresponded with her at great length, and she had sent him a signed photograph with 'All my love, Deanna' on it. All her love, mind. He had it, framed, on the wall of his Deanna Durbin room. His wife, who had been rather a jealous woman, God bless her, had not approved, but now that she had passed on, God rest her soul, he was free to spend as much time with Deanna as he wished. Eve looked forward to seeing more of Arthur Hope and promised to have tea with him soon.

Lord Lucan 2 then got up to thank everyone, and she realised that he was the chairman of the governors.

Expansion and Reduction

On Saturday afternoon Kieron was in the weights room trying to build some muscles. Four of them stood around Mr Avery who was showing them how to lift, stripped to the waist. An oak amongst saplings. Kieron watched as he lay down on the padded bench and pushed the weight into the air, arms outstretched, muscles gleaming and hard. Two giant tree trunks with mossy fur at their bases. The strength impressed and intimidated him.

'Come on, wimps!' Avery sprang to his feet. 'Your go.'

The trouble with being a man was that you had so much to live up to. Kieron looked at Mr Avery, then at Miles who towered above him, then down at his own body. So much of it was luck. He hated his ribs. He loathed the whiteness of his skin and the hairless nipples. The comparisons in the showers were the worst of all, especially with Miles there because he had the biggest and paraded it in front of everyone. The gnawing question was, did it grow any more after the age of fifteen or sixteen? What if it didn't? What if he always had to compete with people like Miles?

Through the slatted window by the door he could see the great pouting blooms of the magnolia tree. He breathed in deeply, filling his lungs and his abdomen. He could see growth everywhere and he wanted to be a part of it.

Shit. This was the last straw. Ecstasy was popping her head round the door and Mr Avery was saying, Come on in, come in and have a go at the weights – I'll show you round! I bet he will. Bastard. Bastard. Fucking bastard. Kieron put his arms across his chest and hugged his shoulders. He looked at his toes and wished he'd gone for a MacDonalds with Willy.

'Well, this is the weights room.' Avery demonstrated a few bits of apparatus to enhance his own. He showed her all his muscles to their best advantage, but Eve was looking at the boys' backs. They were watching Miles. She sensed their embarrassment and felt awkward. Avery was rippling his pectorals. She was looking at Kieron looking at his toes.

'How do you fit everyone in here?' she asked, to break the silence. 'Surely the classes are too large.'

Avery was lost in his own body and was counting to himself.

'It's easy,' said Felix, coming up behind her, having followed her from the library. 'See that?'

Eve's eye followed a track of arbitrarily placed bricks jutting out of the wall ascending to the high ceiling.

'What is it?'

'Climbing practice thing.'

'Surely you can only fit two or three people on that.'

Felix looked at her as though she were naïve.

'Class size is a problem in all subjects. We have our own, age-old solution here. Only Avery is a qualified Games teacher. The rest of us muck in incompetently. So we can expect to have seven or eight boys fall off the climbing thingy per term. That's usually four or five in hospital in traction for a month – reduction in class size of four or five. And you still have the fees. Then there's rugby – good for at least three major injuries per match. Easy.'

Eve looked thoughtful. Kieron Oakey had the most lovely bottom she had ever seen.

Sinking Feeling

The summer time-table was good. You finished lessons at 4.30 sometimes, had tea, then played cricket and stuff until supper. And if you were no good at cricket or injured, you could watch 'Blue Peter' or 'Home and Away' or something, with *more* toast and jam. On Saturdays you could watch them again on video.

Elvis and Coriolanus Smith, a third-former with piles who liked model-making from balsa wood, sat in the basement house common room in chairs with the innards spilling out from the covers. Elvis usually found the easy chairs very difficult because they were difficult to get hold of – there being only five to service sixty-one boys – and because once you'd got one they were very difficult to sit in. You had to manoeuvre your behind into position carefully, and if you were lucky enough to park one cheek comfortably, the other was usually being pranged by a protruding bit of wire. But Elvis and Coriolanus were seated comfortably on two early sixties PVC chairs with no legs (the best) because everyone else was playing cricket or smoking by the bins or chatting up girls in the crypt or in the park.

'Wow!' said the presenter on the television, casting a cursory glance at an enormous papier-mâché castle built by two schoolboys and thrusting a microphone under one of their noses. 'How long did this take to make, Jason?'

'Well...' Jason looked thoughtful. 'Um ... about a month, I suppose, but we really only spent a week on...'

'Great!' The microphone was snatched away from Jason, who hadn't realised the question was largely rhetorical and not meant to be answered.

'Amazing! Well, Hugo, I know you were the one who thought up the idea – what gave you the idea to build a castle?'

Hugo looked self-consciously at the wrong camera, also unaware that his reply was of no consequence to the presenter who was wearing yellow trousers with ants in them.

'Well, I'd been reading a book called...'

'And that's what gave you the idea! Well, I think it's tremendous! I'm afraid that's all we've got time for this week, but I'll be back on Monday to show you how to make a moonscape for your hamsters and gerbils to play in...' (camera shot to woman in avant-garde hairstyle and the voice of an eight year old) '...and you'll find out what happened when Sue and I hang-glided off a cliff in north Devon...' (camera shot to woman in purple) '...and I'll be giving you the results of our competition – see you next week!'

'Bye!'

'Bye-bye!'

'Bye!'

Elvis felt a sinking feeling as the music started. He wanted to see how to make the moonscape for his hamster now, and he wanted them to carry on talking to him. Most of all he liked the women and especially the one with the brown hair and the smiley face. He liked the way she showed her gums and the way she couldn't quite pronounce her 'r's and he liked her necklaces and short skirts and freckles and he wanted to marry her. He poked his finger into a foam gash in the PVC chair, and then went off to make another piece of toast.

Adrian rang. He asked if he could come and see Eve. She had been seeing him for just over a year, when he could fit her in. Usually, when he wasn't lecturing, he spent his time researching, or travelling to hot countries for research into poverty.

'I thought perhaps a quiet evening in with a meal and a video.'

He had spoken. Eve was elated. If she wondered at her own behaviour, scurrying around shopping, slicing and chopping, she pushed such thoughts to the back of her mind. Adrian was coming to dinner and she was going to spoil him.

At a quarter to eight she had just finished arranging slices of avocado and smoked salmon on a bed of lettuce, and was about to shred a huge carrot. The phone rang. It was Adrian.

'Sorry, darling. I can't make it tonight.'

'What do you mean?'

'Something urgent's cropped up.'

'What sort of thing?'

'Meeting with Professor Short.'

'A meeting? Now?'

'Well, they've asked me to dinner – informal sort of thing – nothing special.'

'Dinner?' (Nothing special?)

'Look, I really can't let them down. He's such an important contact – you've no idea. And Bill Gregory's going to be there. You've no idea...'

'When did he ask you?'

'Only about an hour ago, or I'd have let you know.'

'Well, why didn't you ring me an hour ago?' She was beginning to sound petulant. Keep calm. 'OK. Some other time. Thanks for phoning.'

She sat on the floor hugging her knees. She caught her reflection looking dejected in the mirror and stuck her tongue out at it. She made her way slowly into the kitchen and surveyed the awaiting feast. The sirloin steak lay flushed and ready on a plate, the wine was breathing heavily.

Calling

Kieron rang his mother. She asked him what grades he'd got and if he'd remembered to sew his name tags into his new cricket jumper. The loft needed lagging and she would probably have to get Mr Duncan to do it since Kieron's father had left her manless. Oh, and don't forget that cricket jumper. She wasn't made of money.

Elvis rang his mother. There was no answer.

Eve rang Adrian. There was no answer.

Someone rang Eve. She was a filthy bitch and he knew what she wanted … she hung up.

Near Miss

That same evening Kieron was sitting on the wall outside Pearce House feeling gloomy. His mood was juggling with a sense of excitement about the things that could possibly happen and a sense of doom that they almost certainly wouldn't. Miss Swanbrook had seen him at his worst. She wasn't going to initiate anything with him after seeing him and Mr Avery side by side. Who had he been kidding? But who else could there be but Miss Swanbrook? Downleaze College only had girls in the sixth form, and they were all patronising.

Then he saw something quite horrible. As he looked up he saw Willy sauntering down the road. This would normally have been an unappealing sight, but now Willy was walking with a *girl*. He stared. They weren't holding hands or anything, but Willy had been trying to get something out of her hair and they were *laughing* together. Seeing Willy trying to be romantic was disgusting, but seeing Willy succeeding was enough to make you puke. PUKE. They were passing Kieron now and he looked down at some moss on the wall and started to pick at it.

'Hi there!' shouted Willy across the road.

Puke. 'Oh, hi!' shouted Kieron.

Willy must have sensed his friend's disappointment. He looked smug for a while and then turned round after they had passed, cupped his hands to his mouth, and yelled:

'Hey, Kieron! Safeway!'

Kieron looked up and smiled with relief. This little incident had reminded him that things could have been a lot worse. He leapt off the wall with a renewed sense of vigour, and almost knocked over Elvis who sped around the corner with a tearful face.

'Hey, Elvis!'

Elvis carried on running, and disappeared into Pearce House through the boys' entrance.

Kieron followed him into his room. Elvis lay curled up on the bed, hiding his face with his pillow.

'Hey, Elvis. What's the matter?'

'Nothing,' came a small voice from behind the pillow.

Kieron knew Elvis was crying. You could see his frail legs quivering and the erratic rise and fall of his rib-cage. Kieron wanted to put his arm around him, but was afraid Elvis would think he was bent. He stood for a moment, watching him helplessly. Then he put a hand on the warm, gently shaking head. He thought of his hamster that had died two years ago.

'Come on, Elvis. Let's go for a drink.'

Elvis, who was thirteen, had never been asked out for a drink before by anyone older. He lifted a blotchy face and nodded.

Crying's Not for Me

———◆◆◆———

'Coo-ee!'

Eve opened the front door to Debbie's knockings. Now Debbie was going to ruin a perfectly good crisis. Not that sympathy wasn't welcome, but the soothing balm could irritate if applied too soon, and Debbie was not going to give her the optimum wallow allowance.

'You hungry?' she asked.

'Starving – haven't eaten all day,' lied Debbie.

'Fancy a feast?'

'Just lead me to it.'

Debbie lived in the flat upstairs and worked at Bolloms the dry-cleaner's. She had short blond hair, or auburn, or black, wore earrings the size of lampshades and was a dab-hand at removing stains of any sort.

'Coo-ee! It's only me!' she would holler every evening at Eve's door for no special reason. Eve hated it sometimes. She would have just got in the bath or started on a pile of essays or be on the phone . . . 'Cooee!' And then Debbie went to Corfu for ten days and she realised how much she missed it.

Eve explained everything, in an apologetic tone, because she knew her neighbour's reaction would be contemptuous.

'What on *earth* do you see in this dickhead? Why do you let him treat you like this?'

Eve didn't know. She sat quietly, like a child awaiting punishment. Debbie helped herself to a tumbler of red wine. Eve opened another bottle and they polished off both bottles and all of the food.

After the video, Debbie walked over to the table and picked up the giant carrot.

'What has Adrian got that this carrot hasn't?'

Eve smiled and shrugged, 'Affection?'

'Wrong! This carrot has more affection than that git. And it's not the most affectionate of carrots.'

43

She clasped her soft white hands around the carrot and brought it over to Eve.

'Let me put the question another way,' she hiccuped. 'What has this carrot got – let's call him Kevin – what has Kevin the Carrot got that Adrian hasn't?'

'Carotene?'

'Wrong! RIGIDITY. This carrot will never go floppy on you. This carrot will be *consistent*. This carrot has one more quality than Adrian Whatshisthingy. Why look further?'

She trotted into the bedroom to place the new lover on the bed for her friend. Fifteen seconds later she emerged with a new find.

'Twenty-four Extra-Safe. I think that was a bit ambitious, Evie.' She counted them with some difficulty. 'Oh dear, still twenty-four. We're not having much fun here, are we? Still, never mind. There's no time like the present.'

She pulled out a condom, ripped the corner of the packaging with her teeth, and rolled it lovingly down the length of the carrot.

'Kevin is ready and waiting.'

They both spluttered with laughter, and Eve took Kevin into the living room and placed him affectionately on the mantelpiece.

Eve was awoken by a strange singing noise. The light was still on, and she was lying on the sofa. She looked at the clock. It was four o'clock in the morning. There was wine on the carpet and she brought a tea-towel from the kitchen to dab at it ineffectively. She turned out the light and wandered into her bedroom. Debbie was sprawled across it in a motionless cartwheel. She sighed, and went back to the sofa. The singing was getting louder. Eventually she went to the window and peaked out through the curtains.

The rain was thundering at the window-pane, and on the glistening street outside she could make out two familiar figures. Kieron was riding a bicycle in circles outside the house, and little Elvis was sitting on the front basket. The pair of them were singing at the top of their voices:

'Raindrops keep falling on my head
But that doesn't mean my eyes will soon be turning red ... red
Crying's not for me ... for me'

They were out of synch and slurring their words outrageously. Eve blinked. It was Kieron. It was Elvis. She went to the front door.

'Hey! You two!'

Kieron stopped pedalling, and the bicycle fell over into the gutter. She helped them to their feet and told them to keep their voices down, and to come in and dry out. They were drenched.

Now who would have thought you would ever actually get inside Ecstasy's flat. *Invited* into Ecstasy's flat. It was a pity he was not sober because he could have remembered it in more detail. At least he wasn't sick in the sink like poor Elvis. He would never have lived that down. But Elvis didn't mind. He was glad to be looked after. That's all he had wanted all evening. Someone to give him clean warm socks, hot chocolate and hold him close. Miss Swanbrook did all that for Elvis. OK, so there were some advantages in puking up. But not as many as being left in the lounge on your own to have a snoop round.

Everything was cream and peach and there were lots of trendy pictures on the wall including a nude man and woman. He tilted his head sideways to read the books on the shelves. Lives of artists, homoeopathic medicine, car maintenance, poetry, fat dictionaries, novels with strange titles, no sex manuals or anything. And this was weird: on top of the bookcase was an Action Man. She had two empty wine bottles on the floor and one on the table. And *two* glasses. Kieron felt uneasy. There was a tea-towel on the mantelpiece and a packet of condoms. Kieron counted them. Twenty-three. Now he felt very uneasy, and put the packet in his jacket pocket. That would sort her out. She wouldn't be having any more fun tonight without him. So who was here? Why did she still have all her clothes on?

She was still in the bathroom with Elvis. He would be OK to sneak a look in the bedroom. It must be that other door. It brushed over the carpet pile. He stood in the doorway staring at the dark shape on the bed. *It was a naked woman.*

Waltzing on Clouds

It was five o'clock by the time the two inebriates left Eve's flat. She eventually fell asleep at six. At eight-thirty the doorbell rang. She squinted at the clock on the mantelpiece, and went barefoot to the door. It was the Reverend Arthur Hope.

'I do hope I haven't woken you, my dear, but I thought you might like some roses from the garden.'

He was holding a basket full of yellow, pink and apricot roses, but he did not hand them to her.

'Oh, that's really kind of you,' she smiled blearily. Still he did not proffer the basket.

'Well, come in. The place is in a bit of a mess.'

Arthur Hope was delighted with the view of his gnomes from her kitchen window. He talked for an hour over tea in the lounge and told her all about Deanna. He ran through her roles in *Can't Help Singing, First Love, One Hundred Men and a Girl*, and measured the various distances he had been from her in feet and inches. He thought she could wipe the floor with modern stars, but he admitted to a budding interest in Madonna.

Eve loved his company, but she felt a pang of guilt. She should be in chapel, and she felt sure he disapproved. She brought the subject up and apologised.

'Do you know what,' he said. 'They get right up my nose, that lot.'

'What lot?'

'That lot. The God Squad.' He waved his arm vaguely over his shoulder. 'They're all frustrated and phobic. They don't know how to think for themselves. So they go for the whole package deal of Christianity. A whole load of Thou Shalt Nots: it makes them feel comfortable and safe. And righteous. Jesus would've hated them. If he existed, that is.'

'Don't you think he did?'

'Oh ... I've been asked to take the Founder's Day service, and I shall, I suppose. But...' Arthur looked tired, 'I don't know anything any more.'

As he spoke his cup, which he had allowed to droop at an increasing angle, spilled tea over his trousers.

'I'm glad I'm retired.'

Eve went to the kitchen for some paper towels, and Arthur seemed bemused at the damp patch in his loins.

'It's all right!' he shouted, spotting the tea-towel on the mantelpiece. He took it to wipe himself down, and saw the most unusual object. After careful examination of it, he replaced the napkin as Eve returned to the room. What a surprising young lady Miss Swanbrook was. And now she was dabbing at his groin.

As he stood up to go, he clasped her face in his hands and said, 'Do you mind if I give you a kiss, my dear? I'm eighty-five and just an old man. You don't mind, do you?' and he gave her a long, still kiss on the mouth. 'You do so remind me of Deanna.'

She heard him going down the steps to his next door basement flat singing 'Waltzing on Clouds'.

Eve did not know what to do. If she reported the incident, Kieron and Elvis would get into serious trouble. If she did not, her behaviour, if discovered, would seem very unprofessional. She considered telling their housemaster, Mr Cuthburtson. Cuthburtson was a pompous, grey, socky man with a very loud voice and the sort of sense of importance which would lead him either to dismiss the matter entirely with a snort, or to take Very Serious Steps Indeed, depending on who had just won the rugby fixture.

Eve decided to let the matter rest for the time being. Perhaps she would tell Arthur Hope. That would cover herself in an emergency. The worst thing was that Kieron must have seen (she closed her eyes in horror) that dreadful carrot. He must think her ... What must he think her?

But Kieron had not seen Kevin the Carrot at all.

Women in Love

The puzzling thing was, what did lesbians do with condoms? He didn't want to tell Willy about the episode, because Willy would blab it around to everyone and then he'd get into trouble. Or rather, he was itching to tell Willy, but common sense made him hold on for a while. They had got back to the boarding house via the fire escape. No one had noticed. Willy had known about it of course, but had just thought it was a normal pub binge that had ended lateish, and he was a bit pissed off at not having been invited. The main reason for not telling Willy was that he didn't want Willy to know about his ignorance on this matter. There was probably something obvious that lesbians did with condoms and he'd look a right prat if he didn't know. A bit of general musing would be fine though.

They were sitting in Willy's study bedroom doing Willy's prep. Willy was still grumpy about missing a good booze-up, and would have been even worse if he knew what he'd really missed. Kieron had never seen his friend so attentive over work. He was doing a dialogue in French, and Kieron was holding the dictionary. Perhaps if he looked up 'lesbian' ... Oh, '*lesbienne*'. This was a good lead in.

'I wonder what lesbians do. I mean, what do they actually *do*?'

Willy looked up, distracted for the first time in a good half-hour. This comment clearly signalled a break. He put down his unchewed Biro and reached authoritatively up to the shelf above the desk, like a librarian finding a specialist reference book. He pulled down a red box-file marked 'Geography Coursework' and opened it. He leafed through a dozen or so magazines and selected one skilfully, finding the page he wanted with ease.

'Here you go.' He handed it to Kieron.

There was a picture of two naked women sitting side by side, with tongues outstretched, licking each other's faces. Because they were half facing the camera their tongues stuck out almost

48

sideways, making them look like exhausted Labradors. Then there was this article, or story, about them. Rachel and Bettina. Kieron was appalled. And excited. As he read it, he stuck his tongue out sideways as far as it would go. It hurt. He couldn't imagine Miss Swanbrook doing any of that with the girl on the bed. He really couldn't. And there was no mention of condoms.

Then Willy showed him another picture of two naked women. They were embracing each other tenderly, and there was a sort of soft focus on them. You could see the sad, liquidy eyes of the one woman. Kieron thought she was utterly beautiful.

That night he thought of the photograph and substituted Miss Swanbrook for the languid one. That girl who had been on her bed became the other one in the photo, and as he pushed the bedroom door open across the rustling carpet pile, he saw them both, wrapped in each other like two soft animals. He stood and watched them, until eventually they became aware of him and asked him to join them. But he refused, and sat down on the bed instead and watched. He repeated this scene over and over again with variations. Sometimes they begged him to join in, sometimes they were ashamed when they noticed him, and sometimes they never saw him at all. Poor, frustrated Miss Swanbrook. She really did need some helping out. He was glad he only shared his room with Marcus Doyle who was a day-boy. At night he was all alone. In Ecstasy.

Adrian: *Nul Points*

It was Monday, lesson after break. The fifth form's controlled test was over after many weeks, and Eve felt she was playing for time until the end of term, which was still over a month away.

'Let's see you take more risks with the paint. It's too controlled.'

Eve's father had died seven years before. Her most vivid memory of him was after a row in her teens about going to Paris on her own to become an artist. She'd stormed out of the house with a suitcase on wheels which kept falling over: seventeen and misunderstood. She had been standing at the station when she saw her father running towards her through the crowd. She turned and pretended not to see him. But as he came nearer, she saw that in his outstretched arm was her passport. She said, 'Thank you' to his anxious face, and not 'I love you.'

'Please be careful.'

'I promise.'

As the train pulled away she saw him standing, helplessly worried, waving goodbye. The man sitting opposite her had one leg, and she cried into her novel.

She had tried to make up for it by telling her mother she loved her, before it was too late. It became her mission: I love you, Mum. But every time she saw her mother the occasion simply didn't seem to present itself. It was worse than sex or salaries. It was love and it was not discussed. She tried walks in the park, discussing childhood, sentimental films or just hugging her. But inevitably the moments were strait-jacketed by domesticity, the need to discuss the price of cheese or the new dress from M and S which was going to be taken in, taken up or taken back. And so it was always at the end of every visit that she tried to squeeze it in. Have you checked your oil? Yes I love you. Have you got enough petrol? I love you, Mum. It always seemed to slip away.

On the last occasion she just said it.

'Well, drive carefully.'

'I will. I love you, Mum.'

'Would you like a pint of milk to take back with you?'

It wasn't until she was home, when she placed the milk in the fridge next to the two pints she already had, that she saw it was whole milk. Her mother only ever bought skimmed for herself.

'Don't let your brushes get hard. Take care of them, and they'll last forever.'

That evening Eve was guarding the pasta sauce and waiting for Adrian to return with a video. He had been gone so long now that she wondered if he'd stopped off at the university and got waylaid. She looked for the Humanities department in his organiser. She hadn't meant to snoop, but flicking through she caught sight of her own name. Eve. There it was in a list of about thirty names. Hers was towards the end: 'Eve 5.' She frowned. She recognised many of the names before hers as ex-girlfriends, but she didn't recognise the names after hers:

Eve 5

Sara 4

Susanna 8

Jill 2

Camilla 6

Eve's hand started to shake. She didn't know what this was, but it wasn't the number of Christmas cards he'd sent them. Eve fucking five. Surely a man his age couldn't keep a list of . . . ? And who was Susanna? And how come she got eight? And what had poor old Jill done – or not done – to deserve two? He was a mean marker. She deeply resented being five.

Adrian's key was opening the front door, and she flipped the book closed.

'I've no sense of fun?' Eve looked up at the ceiling after a long, circular argument and tried to remember the last time she'd had fun with Adrian.

'Well, basically,' said Adrian, 'I think what all this comes down to is your age, isn't it? You're just that age, aren't you?'

Eve hadn't mentioned the scores she had found. She sat very still, and carried on staring at the ceiling, knowing that, as long as she didn't blink, nothing would show.

'I don't mean that cruelly or anything. I don't want us to split up. It's just that you're bound to just want to get married and have children – at your age, I mean – and I can't possibly have as much *fun* with you as I can with younger girls – women – well, my sort of age.'

Eve felt something snap inside. Not in anger. Perhaps it was an umbilical cord that broke. Keep calm. Ride the storm. He's blown it now so why get upset? Worthless piece of shit. Just don't react.

'I see,' said Eve. 'I'm two years older than you and I'm too old. Is that all?'

Adrian turned a pained face towards her. She got up and left. Eve 5, Adrian nil.

Love Left Standing

Eve looked fat and distorted under water. A small insect clung to the side of the bath in a tidal wave, and she saw her body as a giant sea monster. A tiny remnant of menstrual blood floated past, the fronds of a red sea plant. She reached for something to read and found a folded Tampax leaflet soggy with steam:

'Fig 1: Find a position which feels comfortable to you. Fig 2: Hold the applicator with your thumb and middle finger at the grooved ridges (b).'

Eve lay in the bath and contemplated a future of stilted laughs and brown and beige. Her attempt to make a living as an artist had failed temporarily, but what if it wasn't temporary? She felt homesick for something uncertain. It was the feeling she'd had at the age of four. The strange climbing frames, the bells, the feeling of being watched for the mistakes you would make, primary colours, the smell of polish and sick, rhymes you'd never heard and menacing toilets with half-doors. She wanted to go home to someone.

'*Fig 1: Choisissez une position confortable. Fig 2: Tenez l'applicateur entre la pouce et le majeur à la hauteur des anneaux (b).*'

Was she trying to go home to Adrian? She had always expected too much of love. Was that why she always ignored the initial siren? It was always there: the thing you noticed in the first week which would haunt you later. (With Adrian it had been his banging on the wall in her flat to tell her neighbours to be quiet. Bang bang. Shut up. Bang bang. Did you come? *Her* neighbours, and she liked them.) But you buried it deeply, and it would only surface later.

'*Fig 1: Trova una posizione che ti è commoda.*'

She had always asked too much of love. Kindness, tenderness, excitement, support, laughter. No one could be expected to give you everything. So now she asked for less. She had her friends around the country, women and men: intelligent conversation in Norwich, fun in Brum, empathy in Swansea.

'Fig 1: Finden Sie eine für Sie angenehme und bequeme Stellung.'

She pulled the plug out and watched the insect brush against her before it span in the giant vortex of water. She saw with its eyes the measureless wall of death, the endless body of the sea monster, and she leapt out of the bath in a sudden panic.

Just as you learnt to ask for less and give more, the tide seemed to turn again. Now the more you gave, the more was expected. You weren't fun enough, you weren't slim enough, you weren't patient enough, you weren't wild enough. Enough for what?

Find a position which feels comfortable to you.

She kept running with the passport, arms outstretched, but no one ever got off the train, and she couldn't expect them to.

The Die Is Cast

Tuesday evening. Debbie thrust a pencil and some paper at Eve.

'Here. Write a list of the advantages and disadvantages of a relationship with Adrian. Go on. Five minutes.'

Eve took up the pencil and thought. Under disadvantages she wrote:

- doesn't love me
- never cuddles me
- incapable of giggling
- collects beer-mats
- obsessed with image and status
- reads sci-fi books with characters called 'Zog' and 'Thrug' and finds them interesting
- total lack of sensuality
- no foreplay
- snores
- lies
- finicky about appearances (mine – not his)
- flirtatious and unfaithful (probably – certainly)
- no ability to empathise

She thought she had better stop because she had come to the end of the page. Under advantages she put:

- articulate

She looked at it. It didn't seem to make him very unique. So she added: 'used to love him'.

She handed the paper to Debbie and said she had lots of marking to do.

'Not until we've exorcised Adrian Gitface. Come on, have some more.' She poured Eve a giant glass of red wine and made her wait in her flat until she got back from Spudulike.

Eve went to fetch her marking and sat down at Debbie's kitchen table. But she was distracted. She found a die in Debbie's fruitbowl and threw it. If she got a six she was doing the right thing leaving

Adrian. (She got a three.) If she got a three she was doing the right thing leaving Adrian. (She got a five.) Perhaps the system was a bit loaded with failure.

After a stuffed potato and another bottle of wine, she put her head down on the table and sighed miserably, 'I haven't done my marking.'

'Come on,' said Debbie, 'let's do it together.'

She opened the top sketch book which was covered with ink diagrams.

'Sanderson – God, his writing's a mess.'

Eve threw the die.

'Six. OK. Six out of ten,' Debbie wrote it in fat felt tip at the bottom of the page. 'Now Ogilvie...'

Eve threw the die again.

'Two,' said Debbie. 'Sorry, Ogilvie. That's life.' She wrote it in, and Eve threw again. 'Kieron Oakey ... three.'

'No – add six for having a nice bottom.'

Debbie chewed this one over, 'OK, then, nine. Nice Bum ... Let's just add "NB." Don't want him getting too cocky. Now ... Ramsbottom ... one ... let's add two for neat writing on the front.'

'And four for being called Ramsbottom,' added Eve. 'It must be a lot to live with.'

'Good thinking. Ramsbottom, this is your lucky day...'

Wednesday. Eve had been teaching for fifty minutes of the double lesson before break. Now she had given them a short exercise to do and she would have five minutes to herself to think.

She had phoned Adrian and he had been out, or not answering. She had seen herself this morning in the mirror by the window. The light had poured in because it faced east, and had shown up every new wrinkle. She had been horrified at the pasty unevenness of her complexion. Her hair was a mess. She had grasped a handful of fat on her thigh. She was getting chubby. No, she was fat, ugly and revolting. It was no wonder Adrian pretended to be out. No wonder. No wonder.

Kieron was aware of Miss Swanbrook's perfume. He sat in front of her and looked up for a moment, chewing the end of his pen as if thinking hard on the exercise. He saw her there, on the bed, her dark hair a silken mass across the pillow, his head buried in it. He saw her pink and gasping. He looked at her downy arms folded on the desk, the blue velvet eyes fixed on the middle distance, and the soft tendril that fell down from her pinned-up hair. She was the most beautiful woman he had ever seen.

Nose

Kieron was sitting outside the headmaster's office. The secretary's small dog was biting at his ankles, and he gave it a smart kick while she wasn't looking. The head was really keeping him waiting: it had been twenty minutes now. The dog launched himself vengefully at Kieron's sock and tore a bite-sized hole in it. At last the door opened and the chairman of the governors came out holding three golf-balls.

'See you on Saturday, then,' he was saying. The headmaster beamed at his secretary and called out, 'All right then, Daphne?' Daphne blushed. Why were heads so *nice* to their secretaries and so vile to everyone else?

He pushed the door and stood aside to let Kieron in, his face re-set to the vile important person look. He motioned to Kieron to sit down and examined some notes in front of him.

'Five detentions in five weeks. What has happened to you, Oakey?'

'Dunno, Sir.'

'And none last term.'

This didn't seem to require a reply, so Kieron gave none.

'Two for bad or missing work, one for possession of alcohol, one for bad language and one for ... *forgetting a sketchbook*?'

'It was the third time I'd forgotten, sir. And I swore very badly.'

The head frowned. Kieron looked at the arm of the chair. It was as shiny as a mirror and the whole room smelt of polish.

'Have you any idea how much your parents pay for you to come here?'

Why bring them in? He hadn't asked to come to this dump. He'd rather be at home watching 'Neighbours' and 'Blackadder' like everyone else. Even at prep school he'd missed 'Blue Peter'. It was a matter of deep resentment that he'd never been able to make a tie-rack out of cornflake packets or a Filofax for his teddy. Like everyone else. Not that he wanted to now, of course. *But* ... he felt deprived. If they didn't want to pay his fees, fine.

'How much do they pay, sir?'

The head looked very vile now, and Kieron reflected that people who didn't have a lot of money always found talking about it offensive – almost like swearing.

'An awful lot – money you apparently don't deserve.'

Deserve? He hadn't seen any of it. Why didn't they save it in the Halifax for him and pay him a lump sum at eighteen instead? He knew about lump sums and he wanted one. Then he could buy a 750cc bike *and* a house and a car and watch television any time he wanted after four p.m. and probably meet girls.

Despite this oversight, the headmaster was obviously a really brilliant man. He had this picture behind him of himself at Oxford and oars on the wall.

'The fact is I'm not going to give up on you that easily.'

He wasn't a bad man really. Kieron noticed he had black hairs sprouting from his nose.

'You've clearly fallen in with a bad lot this term, or you're going through an adolescent crisis.'

Now he was trying to be all liberal. What was an adolescent crisis anyway? Who invented this crap? Kieron was sure it was some adult plot aimed at humiliating you, to hide their jealousy of your firm young bodies. He didn't know anyone who'd experienced anything more than bodily changes in adolescence and, let's face it, the head was still having those in his nose – pretty rapidly. Kieron wondered if he plucked them ever, and how old he would be before he started getting hair in his own nose.

'Is there anything bothering you at the moment?'

'No, sir.' Did it tickle?

'Whatever it is that's caused this uncharacteristic behaviour, I'm going to give you a chance to put it behind you.' He was speaking slowly, measuring his words. 'But only because it is uncharacteristic. I'm going to let you turn over a new...'

While the head thought about the next word, Kieron wondered if he had turned into a rebel at last. When he used to play on the swing his sister would come home from school, give him a Chinese burn and tell him to bog off so she could play on the swing with her friends. He always went.

'...leaf.'

He showed Kieron out, telling him he could start by getting a decent pair of socks.

Labelled

On Friday Eve had just enough time to grab a bite to eat and go shopping before Activities began at two-thirty. She visited the nearest baker's shop to the school and bought herself a Cornish pasty, then she went in search of a nearby park bench. She hadn't eaten since her cursory nibble of the Spudulike, and she wanted to eat the pasty whole. She still felt empty and abstracted about the Adrian incident, but the hot sun seemed to be trying to breathe some life into her. A butterfly even fluttered around her wrists, and for a moment she smiled. She raised her arm quickly, but she hadn't hit a Red Admiral or a Cabbage White. Dangling from her sleeve was a label: 'Dorothy Perkins £24.99 Size 10.'

She sat down on a bench, took out the pasty and bit off so much of it that she was unable to chew.

'Hello,' said Kieron, approaching from her left. He had followed her from school and tried to look surprised. 'Fancy meeting you here.'

Eve tried to say hello, but only an 'Mmm' came out.

'Don't you like eating in the canteen, then?'

'Mmm,' Eve gave a sort of not-bothered-either-way tone to her mooing.

Kieron sat down beside her and tried to think of something else to say. She had a large crumb to one side of her top lip, and he longed to brush it away. He felt he was staring at it so he looked down, down her long throat to where a gold pendant heart glided on a lucky chain at her cleavage.

'Cleavage,' he said.

'Mmm?'

Kieron's stomach lurched. He couldn't believe what he'd just said.

'Mr Cleavage – runs the catering – don't blame you for not eating there.'

Eve managed to get a purchase on the lump of pasty and started chewing manically.

'Did your boyfriend give you that locket?'

Eve shook her head, still chewing. 'Mmm mmm,' she said, shaking her head.

'Who did then?'

She parted her lips at last and breathed out a long relieved sigh.

'Oh, I bought it myself.'

Kieron looked pleased, although he wondered if there was a picture of anyone in the locket. She was arranging her bags and looked as if she might be about to make a move. He looked back up to her mouth: the crumb was still there. All he had to do was reach out and stroke it away.

'You must find it boring teaching here,' he said, hoping to keep her a little longer while he worked up the courage.

'Well ... no, not really.' The lips moved softly and her eyelids almost closed on her cheeks in the sun. 'I don't get much free time, though.'

'What do you do in your free time?' (Ready, steady, *now*. Brush it off. Go on.)

She tilted her face toward the sun. 'That's the thing – I don't get any.'

'Well, what are you doing tonight?' He pulled a face at his own clumsiness. That must've sounded like a chat-up line. He was still wincing when she turned to him and said, 'I'm seeing your father. I thought you knew. He can't make parents' day so he wants a word about your future.'

Kieron looked shocked. He dreamt about her, longed for her, followed her every move, and his father just asked her out like that.

'Of course I knew – I forgot.'

'Anything you want me to say about you?'

'No.'

He looked at the hedge opposite and bit his lip. The conversation seemed to have tailed off, so he tried to revive it.

'I'm not in detention this week – you could tell him that.'

'Neither am I.'

'Really?'

'I'm supposed to be singing with the girls' house at this Old Boys' reunion.'

Kieron was filled with more panic. Cuthburtson had asked

people from his house to wait at tables for the reunion dinner, and he hadn't volunteered. He would volunteer as soon as he got back.

'Oh that,' he said. 'I'm going to that.'

'Are you?'

'Mmm. Waiting at tables, you know, stuff like that.'

'What's it like?'

'Dunno. I've never been before.'

She was getting up to go now and he leapt up to help her.

'Let me carry your bags for you.'

'There's nothing in them yet. Thanks anyway.'

'Well, let me walk you to the shops – I can carry your bags back for you.'

'I'm going clothes shopping, actually. I've got nothing smart to wear for this do on Saturday.'

Kieron pictured her undressing in cubicles, but she was already walking away from him, and he felt desperate.

'Miss Swanbrook!' he called after her.

'What?' She turned.

'See you this afternoon, then.'

'OK.' She turned back and started to walk away.

'Miss Swanbrook!'

'Yes?'

'Just a tip.'

'What?'

'If you buy a new dress, take the tag off first.'

She smiled and turned to go, the pasty crumb still on her lip.

On Friday afternoons it was Activities. Most of the school dressed up as soldiers or naval cadets and strutted up and down the quadrangle until tea-time. This was the day when Felix wore his khaki camouflage outfit and shouted a lot. He stamped about, secure in the knowledge that he could merge into the undergrowth should the enemy take a notion to invade Downleaze College fields.

A few boys and most of the sixth-form girls gave this a miss, opting for community service instead. Kieron had opted to join Miss Swanbrook's small group to visit the centre for the homeless in Folly's Yard. Most of the boys who joined were liberal-minded or flat-footed, and Kieron was angry when Willy joined because Willy had always loved dressing up as a soldier and playing with guns.

It was such a shock to the system, this dreadful place full of drunks. Well, they weren't all drunk, but they looked pretty scruffy. And the *smell*. Kieron had never seen anything like Folly's Yard. Willy had doubled up holding his nose, and Kieron had stood shell-shocked as Miss Swanbrook went briskly about her business, seemingly unaware of any stench. She must have had a very insensitive smell system. She didn't flinch when a man with matted hair and an empty beer bottle tottered up to her and slammed her on the back. Kieron was about to go and save her, but she seemed to know him, smiled, and called him 'Dan'.

She led them to a small kitchen with a hatch out on to a large room. A youngish man with a beard was buttering rolls and greeted Miss Swanbrook.

'Hello, Nigel.' She seemed pleased to see him. 'I've brought some new recruits.'

Nigel, what a pathetic name, Willy had said. Fancy being called Nigel and having a beard and buttering rolls for smelly people. He wasn't coming again.

Within twenty minutes she had them all busy, stirring powdered soup into water and serving people at the hatch. You sort of got used to it after a while and you felt safe behind the hatch. Not that these were bad people or anything. They were just poor. Probably they had turned to drink and lost all their money. Willy said they were all lazy slobs scrounging off tax-payers' money. They were probably well qualified, or could have been. They hadn't had to drink, and now they expected us to fork out for them. He wasn't wasting any more of his afternoons doing this for them and putting up with their smell. But Miss Swanbrook had heard him and gone up the wall. She gave him such a talking to, you wouldn't think her capable. And Willy looked all downtrodden then. You had to admit, actually, that it was sort of hard to imagine Dan as an ex-manager of Nat West or something.

Then when everyone was fed and the washing up was done and you thought it might be time to go home early, she had something else up her sleeve.

'Go and talk to them. Go on. They don't bite.'

Talk about what? You can't just talk to people. Kieron had gone over to a raggedy man in the corner smelling of urine, with purple veins in his face. He asked him his name, where he was from and if he liked it here. He was Joe, and he asked Kieron all about himself, and Kieron talked. He liked the man's watery eyes and felt suddenly ashamed. He was ashamed of his uniform and the thousands spent on his education. Far more ashamed than when the head had tried to shame him down his pointy nose.

Food for Thought

Mr Oakey had invited Eve out for a pizza that evening. It was ostensibly to thank her for teaching his son, but also to discuss Kieron's future, or, at least, this was what he told Kieron. But when he said, 'It's only to discuss your education. Don't look at me like that. There's no need to read anything into it – you can come too if you like,' he hadn't reckoned on Kieron taking him up on it, and the atmosphere at the restaurant was tense.

Mr Oakey took Eve's coat and insisted on hanging it up properly. (Now he would know she was the sort of woman with *bits* on her collar.) Kieron spilt some water, and Mr Oakey called him a clumsy clot.

'It's all right,' said Eve. 'It's only a little. I've got some tissues in my bag.'

She opened it and a white sheaf of Sainsbury's receipts fluttered across the table like a dove from a magician's hat. And three coloured Kleenex tissues *with bits of fluff on them*. (Now he would know she was the sort of woman who kept her tissues for two years.) And then the strangest thing happened.

Something traced a curly path around her ankle. It circled slowly, then worked its way up her calf and inserted itself in the fold behind her knee. It was, unmistakably, a shoeless toe. She looked across at Mr Oakey: he was setting aside the soggy tissues and studying the wine list with minor irritation. She looked at Kieron: he was playing with the salt-cellar and looking mortified.

'Now, what would you like to drink?' asked Mr Oakey, smiling (a sensuous smile?).

'A mineral water would be fine.'

The toe moved gently around to the front of her calf, and proceeded to tease with a series of gentle brushstrokes using the rest of the toes and the lap of the foot.

'I'll have a lager,' said Kieron.

She looked at him, but he was studying the menu on a board behind him.

'Are you sure you won't have a bottle of wine with me?' Mr Oakey smiled gently at her.

The foot swivelled round to the front of her calf.

'No – no, I'm driving.'

He ordered, composed, his face betraying nothing of a straying foot. Kieron turned round muttering, 'A Four Seasons pizza with garlic bread,' as if food were a source of shame. He gloomily stroked the salt-cellar. The foot stroked the inside of her ankle. He turned the salt-cellar round on its pedestal. The toe slid up to her inside leg above the knee, and she felt her insides curl into a ball of pleasure.

The meal ordered, Mr Oakey leant forward and looked at Eve: 'Now, what I want to know is, is he good enough for Art at university? Are we talking the Slade or something? He's good at telling me he's good, but I want to know from you.'

Kieron hid his face in his hands.

'I mean, I know he likes *you*, but does he like Art?'

Kieron's horror was complete, and Eve dared not look at him. She was aware that he was wincing, and the continuation of the frolics under the table made it inconceivable that he was the owner of the foot. But Mr Oakey was hiding things well. He spent the next twenty minutes talking about UCAS, references and university entrance requirements.

At the end of the meal they waited a long time for the bill but it did not arrive, so Mr Oakey got up to go and pay. At that moment, the foot business stopped.

'Thank you for being nice about me in front of him,' said Kieron when he had gone. 'He always treats me as if I'm about seven when he sees me. I half expect him to produce packets of Smarties from his pockets.'

'I'm sorry it's been embarrassing for you.'

'It has. But ... what he said about me liking you and that, it's true, I do like you...'

'Here comes your father.'

Kieron sighed. 'Oh yes. Here he comes. *In his laced-up shoes.*'

Eve stared at Kieron, but he was putting on his jacket and humming.

'Right, let's go!' said Mr Oakey. 'Can we give you a lift?'

'No thanks. My car's just around the corner.'

'Then we'll walk you to it.'

Kieron was looking at her carefully now: an intent, fearless stare. She turned her eyes away, in case he saw in them something she didn't know herself. She talked to him about graphic design or something.

Winning

The following day was parents' day. Kieron's father had flown to Hong Kong that morning, and Kieron stood watching some warm-up cricket with Elvis before going into the big hall. Elvis's face looked tearfully smudgy again, and Kieron asked him what the matter was.

'I hate Cuthburtson!' he said, relieved to be able to confide in someone.

'We all do,' said Kieron, twirling a cricket ball under his forefinger.

'Yes, but I'm going to kill him. I'm going to *kill* him!'

It was unusual to see Elvis gritting his teeth. It was almost frightening. He pictured Elvis and Cuthburtson squaring up to each other for a fight, Elvis gritting his teeth and Cuthburtson slain with a single small stone from Elvis's sling.

'What's brought this on, then?'

'He's a bastard!' spat Elvis, biting his lip suddenly to stop it trembling. 'He's always punishing me and I haven't done anything wrong.'

'He's a sadist,' said Kieron. Elvis nodded gravely, but frowned. He had always thought Mr Cuthburtson was a Conservative.

Kieron's parents were not playing their role. His mother was on holiday with her new man, and his father would visit Kieron the following week on his birthday. He had invited Kieron to stay at his nearby flat for two days while he was in the country. Kieron watched the other boys' parents talking to Ecstasy and wished he could have stood with his own mother and father to watch her at close range.

Elvis was really down. His mother had said she was coming and then at the last minute had phoned to say something had 'cropped up'. It wasn't fair. She never phoned Elvis except to make arrangements. Or break them. He and Kieron stood around proffering sherry on trays ('Dry or sweet?'). Kieron watched the mothers with their all-year tans and throats heavy with gold. He was glad his mother hadn't come really. She would have called him 'Darling' in front of people and gone on and on at him for not doing well. It was probably just as well she wasn't there. It really was.

Elvis watched the mothers in their silks and cashmeres, all soft and perfumed. He would never forgive his mother for not coming. Never.

The day of the inter-house cricket match finals was treated as a special occasion, and it was made to coincide with the fifth- and sixth-form parents' day to increase the number of spectators. One or two local dignitaries and old boys also made an effort if the weather was fine.

It was a clear blue day and the parents were milling around the pavilion sipping tea, the mothers in wide-brimmed hats, the fathers incidental and in search of alcohol. Eve had been standing alone for some time when a kindly, red-faced man approached her. This was Mr Widgerow, one of the wealthiest men in the area. He owned a lot of property in the town and had donated a vast sum to the college's appeal fund. Eve thought he was the groundsman, and she was grateful to this man with his friendly local burr for making her feel less conspicuous. But Mr Widgerow did not render her less conspicuous in the eyes of the headmaster's wife, and he did not have the same calming effect on her as he did on Eve. She approached, her thin lips spreading across her face towards him, her eyes sparkling at Eve like a new scalpel. Eve watched her with amazement, and realised her mistake. The headmaster's wife could not be called a social climber. She was a mountaineer. You couldn't help feeling that in her handbag she was concealing gleaming crampons.

Her ascent was interrupted by a yell from the cricket pitch. Miles Frayling came running off, his face covered in blood.

'I've broken my nose!' he squealed at the housemaster, Mr Cuthburtson. 'Sir, sir! Help!'

Eve dashed over to him. Mrs Frayling, who had run up shouting 'Darling!', now stood back shrieking at her son to mind where he dripped his blood. Her dress had cost a fortune and money didn't grow on trees. Elvis thought she must have forgotten about their flat in New York and the cottage in Corsica, or else they had fallen on hard times.

'For God's sake, Frayling! Get back on the pitch!' shouted Cuthburtson.

'But, sir, I've broken my nose! Please, sir!'

'Well, you're not going to break it again, are you? Get on the pitch and play for your house!' Then he added, by way of encouragement, 'For God's sake, boy, we're *winning*!'

Matron sidled up, indifferently, with an aspirin.

Brand New Heartache

Kieron had to wait a full week for the opportunity of seeing Ecstasy outside lesson time again. There had been few sightings of her since the meal out: perhaps he had been too forward. There was so much he had to say to her, he just needed the chance. He wasn't sure what, exactly, but he felt sure he could prove himself to her somehow. The days dragged, and everything seemed to be focused on Saturday night.

The old boys' reunion was to take place in the Lockwood-Pryce building, a new construction resembling a spaceship which seemed to have landed on a roof next to the chapel. Lockwood-Pryce was an OD (Old Downleazean) architect who, having been made redundant in the recession, had gone to work abroad. There he became a millionaire and, whilst making no money for his country, managed to make a name for himself at one of its most cherished institutions by endowing the college with five designer egg-shaped domes of glass, too cold in winter and blisteringly hot in summer. It was reserved for visitors because the furnishings were the only smart ones in the school. Kieron had never been inside the construction before and Eileen, an assistant caterer, advised him to wear something cool for waiting at tables. He hovered around the long table reserved for ODs from Pearce House, adjusting his tie.

'Don't you worry too much about your tie, lover. You'll be wondering why you bothered by the end of the evening, I can tell you.' Eileen gave him a knowing look and dumped a pile of serviettes in his arms. Her plump arm brushed his and she went off pinkly in her zip-up nylon overall, carrying with her the secrets of past evenings under the five eggs. Kieron watched her go into the kitchen, which he half expected to revolve into the room revealing a control panel and the crew of the Starship Enterprise; but it didn't.

At eight o'clock the first groups began to arrive from the various boarding houses, where they had been having sherry and bumping into each other after a decade or two. Many of the Pearce House men were quite young, Kieron thought, and there were a couple of older members of staff from each house to remind them of the Good Old Days. After he and Eileen had served the starter, Kieron stood back to have a look at his table. Nearest to him were three young men in their late twenties, already quite drunk, talking rowdily to each other and occasionally to mobile phones. In the middle of the table were four slightly older men in their thirties and forties. He recognised one of them as a newscaster from television, and another as a Conservative MP. At the far end of the table were some much older men and, sandwiched between them, some masters, laughing too loudly at jokes to be convincing and swapping useful addresses feverishly on pieces of napkin. Looking rather isolated at the end of the table, Kieron recognised a soft-faced actor who was well known for his tomato ketchup advertisements.

At around a quarter past eight, the headmaster entered. Everyone stood up with a scraping of chairs, and the retired chaplain, Mr Hope, said grace. Kieron circled the table, overhearing fragments of conversation.

'Foxes are small fry.'

'OK, but aren't deer illegal?'

'God, don't be tedious, Jasper. When you see the look in a stag's eye when it's cornered – now that's a prize for you. My God, real pride and defiance.'

Kieron hoped things would improve. He could see the guests at the High Table: Mr Hope, Cuthburtson and Mr Cox, the present chaplain, who was trying to have a conversation with a confused-looking cricket star. But there was no sign of Ecstasy at any of the tables. He gloomily distributed Beef Wellington to a man who was trying to impress a visiting American academic.

'After my Radio Four play, I was swamped with letters.'

'Radio *foreplay*? My God ... we never have that kinda thing in the States. What happens?'

'Well it starts with this woman's monologue – her husband's left her and she just talks for the first five minutes ...'

'What? I mean, are there sound-effects, or what?'

'Oh, yes! It's not just her talking. To tell the truth I wasn't very impressed with the sound.'

'Jesus! You know, you English, you crease me up,' said the American, shaking his head. 'I mean, you seem so kinda ... stuck up, in some ways. Like this kinda do.' He looked around, indicating all the black ties and cummerbunds. 'And then, my God, radio foreplay!'

'Hey, fag!' One of the younger members of the group threw a cork at Kieron from the end of the table: 'Call this service? My glass has been empty for at least two seconds. Another six bottles, I think, and not this "Downleaze College 1994" plonk either!' They started mentioning quality wines, and Kieron went to the kitchen trying to remember one of them.

'Take them round the back,' said Eileen, handing him a crate of Châteauneuf-du-Pape. 'Marcie'll cork them for you.'

'I can do it myself, don't worry.'

'No. You take them to Marcie, there's a love,' and she gave him a wink.

Kieron found Marcie, a chunky woman with orange hair, crouching on an empty crate and pouring wine through a funnel. Her bare white legs straddled the crate, and he watched as she decanted the good wine into some empty Ribena bottles and filled the good bottles with a mixture of a cut price supermarket wine, Ribena and water.

'Won't they notice?' he asked.

Marcie rubbed her nose. 'Nah ... it's after nine o'clock. They don't know their arse from their elbow by half-past eight. Any road, there'll be a bottle of Ribena for *you* to take home, love, if you get my meaning.'

As he came out he passed the chaplain leaning against the wall in the kitchen with headphones on and scribbling on a notepad. He wondered fleetingly if some message of arrival were being relayed from the girls' boarding house singing group, but looking over Mr Cox's shoulder he saw, 'Brown-eyed Girl, 3 o'clock, 14:1.'

It was a long, thankless evening and, but for the occasional glass of wine Eileen slipped him between courses, Kieron was not enjoying himself. The noise was unbearable. Things began to blur a little. The three younger men started to call him 'Fagette', the men from Mitchell House started throwing bread rolls around the hall, and the tomato ketchup man slapped his bottom. There was a sudden roar followed by a hush as a lump of cheesecake smacked on to the domed glass ceiling and stayed there. Miss King took advantage of the momentary silence to announce the new girls' house singing, 'A medley of songs old and new.'

They had appeared from nowhere like foxes. Kieron stood

motionless as Ecstasy in violet blue, twelve girls and Miss King opened their mouths to sing, and the sweet sound of 'Dreaming' by the Everly Brothers wafted over the tables. Even though she herself would have preferred the classics, Miss King had carefully selected the songs to bring back memories for each generation of old boy.

'I can make you mine, taste your lips of wine,
Any time, night or day.
Only trouble is, Gee wiz,
I'm dreaming my life away...'

There was a rowdy applause as the first song ended, and one or two obscene comments were drowned by wolf-whistles. The girls looked embarrassed and Kieron felt uncomfortable for them, but the second song followed quickly.

'"I can't help falling in love with you",' announced Miss King, not looking at anyone in particular.

It was beautiful. The girls stood in two rows, all different shapes and sizes, in blue skirts with white tops, flanked at one end by violet blue and by brown and beige at the other. As they sang in harmony they seemed to become one, one big blob of sweet femininity. Kieron loved them all. But he loved one of them above all else in the world. He loved her so much he had to blink back what seemed almost like a tear. He realised he was still clutching a tray full of wine as someone from his table started snatching the bottles from it.

'Wise men say only fools rush in,
But I can't help falling in love with you...'

He turned round apologetically, but they had all filled their glasses and were gawping at the group of singers, except for the ketchup man who was staring wistfully at Kieron.

The end of the second song was followed less by applause than by total pandemonium. Some people cheered, some roared obscene suggestions, some started stamping on the floor for more, and one table started throwing the paper carnations from the decorative table centrepiece. Kieron watched the faces of the singing team grow red with confusion. The neat ranks began to flutter. Miss King said something to Miss Swanbrook and then they stood back in positions ready, it seemed, for the next song. Then suddenly a man in the next group to Kieron's jumped up on the table and began gyrating his hips at the singers and shouting, 'Phwoar! Get ya tits out!'

Kieron looked from Miss King to Miss Swanbrook, and for the first time he was struck by a similarity of look in their faces. They were not unlike the deer he had heard about earlier, hunted into a corner by a pack of hounds. Both looked back at their attackers with defiance and dignity, and he could see that nothing the yapping dogs could do to them would weaken the nobility of these gentle creatures. He looked back at the deerhunters to see if they were valiant. They seemed too drunk to know what they had done. The man on the table was still gyrating obscenely, and Kieron wanted to go up to him and drag him on to the floor.

'Stop it! Get off that table!'

'Who are you?'

But before he could object, Kieron had thrown him tumbling to the ground, a weak, contrite drunkard. Everyone applauded; order was restored. The women glowed with gratitude and continued to sing, especially for him, for Kieron.

Only Kieron found that he was standing on the same spot, and hadn't moved. He hadn't made the two paces towards the adjacent table and he hadn't told the man to get down. He had stood by and watched. He had let a moment of true heroism pass him by, an unrepeatable opportunity. Then he realised there was still time. The seconds passed, uncomfortably. He could still do it. The man was still making rude gestures, the atmosphere was becoming more tense and uncontrolled. Everyone was looking in his direction. The audience was his, the opportunity would never repeat itself ... At that moment he felt something wet on his head. He reached up and found that a piece of cheesecake had fallen from the ceiling and a soggy strawberry decorated his hair.

The retired chaplain stood up and went over to the group of singers. Someone shouted something rude about cassocks and he accompanied them out through the glass doors. Kieron watched Ecstasy's flaming face bringing up the rear as she got caught in the rotating doors and circled twice. He followed her violet blue hips as they disappeared down the corridor. He could have wept.

At around midnight he made his way to the toilets which were outside and across the quadrangle. (Lockwood-Pryce hadn't thought that one through.) In his mind he went over and over what he could have done, but hadn't. He was just passing the side of the chapel when the headmaster, who was coming down the path towards him, suddenly ducked and disappeared into the shadows of the wall. He heard footsteps and looked round to see the headmaster's wife marching up the steps to the Lockwood-Pryce building, her heels hitting the granite like ice-picks. He carried on, and saw the headmaster hiding behind a buttress, his back flat against the wall.

'Hello, sir,' said Kieron.

'Hello,' said the headmaster, suddenly examining the stone-work. 'This stone is crumbling ... dreadful.'

Kieron made his way back to the hall and passed a trouserless figure. It was the statue of the college founder. He was wearing a white shirt and dickie bow, and had an After Eight stuck to his nose. Kieron stood awhile in the cool air and shared the indignity of the century-old man. He thought he would collect his wine from Marcie and go to bed.

Not Time's Fools

On Wednesday the tall easels were out and everyone was standing for an ink wash of a collection of leafy plants. Eve watched their thoughtful profiles, and recalled something which had shocked her some days before.

She had been in Arthur Hope's dining room recovering from the ordeal of the reunion, and she had studied the sepia photographs on the wall. In each one stood a remarkably striking young man: clean-shaven, straight-backed, with a warm half-smile. With his creamy skin and open face he was all youth. And yet this person was unmistakably Arthur Hope, an old man with white fur in his ears and hands like two small roast chickens. It was the eyes which gave him away: his whole essence was there. From them crept out the same playful warmth which she could see wholly unchanged across the tea-trolley.

Smallwood put his hand up for help and she went over to rescue his dripping wash. Smallwood was fifteen and looked fifty-five. When he was fifty-five he would feel more comfortable about himself and look more natural. He would be a finicky manager of something-or-other and make clever remarks with classical references which undermined his employees. She prowled around pretending to observe the paintings, studying the profiles of her fifth form intently.

Stephen Bingle would put on weight. He would have a large jowl, but he would always be taking orders from others. Willy Page would be something in the business world, but definitely a wheeler-dealer, with a cache of girly magazines, a pot belly and an unhappy wife. Miles would look distinguished with grey temples and grey suits, but he would remain a doer, not a thinker. He would marry someone cleverer than himself and feel inadequate. Roland Jones would get thinner and thinner and resemble an earnest missionary, which he probably would be. Selby, who had a couple of hang-ups because his father owned a couple of islands, would continue to punish himself. He would vehemently support all lost causes, live off canned soup and have a wardrobe full of odd socks. Kieron Oakey would look ... how would he look? His hair would recede, he might even be bald, and he would be ... what would he be? She walked to the other side of his easel and tried to get a new angle on him. She tried him in a few situations: poet, artist, bricklayer, Nobel prize winner, lollipop man, unemployed architect, street actor. He could be any of them, and he would never lose his essential Kieron Oakiness, his imagination and his coy humour. She repeated the exercise for thirty and eighty years old, and still Oakey emerged unscathed. Then she had them toddling around her in romper suits. She wanted to pick them all up and take them home.

It was a shame Time killed so many opportunities. It seemed all the men deemed appropriate for her were sooner or later obsessed with the speed of her deterioration these days, when Arthur Hope at eighty-five and Kieron at fifteen saw only a woman they treasured. They weren't Time's Fools.

The bell went suddenly and no one had put their things away. She realised she hadn't been keeping her eye on the clock.

That evening Mr Oakey was back over from Hong Kong on a 'flying visit' before going on to London. It was Kieron's birthday on Thursday, he said, but, having missed parents' day, he was anxious to speak to Kieron's tutor, so he arranged to meet Miss Swanbrook for a quick drink that Wednesday evening in a quiet wine bar he knew.

Divorced and dapper, he looked charming by candlelight. His Kieron-like eyes glinted sadly as he outlined how impossible it was to visit his son very often. Perhaps it was a pleasurable feeling that he liked her, or a curiosity about Kieron that made Eve agree to go back to his town flat for coffee.

She entered a spacious room, sparsely but expensively furnished. There were no clues on the mantelpiece to any kind of life lived here. Just a half-empty packet of cigarettes and some paperclips. In a corner, stacks of newspapers and photograph albums. She fished out an old-looking one ('Black or white?' from the kitchen. 'White! No sugar!') and flicked through it backwards. There was the ex-Mrs Oakey, brown and handsome, standing with Mr Oakey on a tennis court somewhere hot. And there was another picture of her, in evening-wear. Lots of the couple together showing lots of teeth. There didn't seem to be any of

Kieron. She went back several pages towards the front of the album. There he was. A small child standing on a beach with his back to the camera. Turning round, frowning, puzzled. Eve traced the face and the shoulders, stroking them. Poor Kieron.

Graham Oakey came in with the coffee and she snapped the album shut.

'Wow! That dates back a bit!' he laughed. 'My share of the divorce booty, that little lot, I'm afraid. I'll show you some of my apartment in Hong Kong. You know, you really ought to come out if you've never been there. You'd love it.'

He rummaged in the corner for some photographs, and then sat very close to her on the settee. So close, that his slow peck on the cheek did not seem unreasonable.

A loud crash made them both turn towards the door. Kieron stood there, glaring at Eve for several seconds.

'Hello, Miss. Glad to see you're getting on,' and he disappeared. They heard the front door slam.

'Don't know what he's doing here now,' said Mr Oakey, only a little ruffled. 'I asked him for a birthday supper tomorrow. Sorry about that. Adolescence is a funny time.'

More Calling

The phone rang. Eve had her tape recorder ready. But it was Felix, asking if she would like to go round and see his slides from the Far East.

Elvis rang his mother to tell her he'd been given A minus in Art. She said How Wonderful but she was entertaining just now and she'd ring him later. She didn't.

Eve rang Adrian to tell him he'd left two pullovers and a sock in her wardrobe and to say someone had been giving her funny calls. He said How Awful, had she told the police?

Eve phoned the police who told her to make a note of the time and date of the calls and, when she had ten to fifteen per month, to ring them back.

The phone rang in Eve's flat:

'I know what turns you on. You're afraid of what I've got to offer, aren't you? What you want is another woman, isn't it? I've seen you with women. I know...'

Eve switched the tape recorder on.

Last Straw

———◆———

That was the last fucking straw. But no, to top it all, Miles had just said to him in the breakfast queue (*and* on his birthday):

'Hey, did you hear about Willy's new girl?'

'No. Who is she?' Panic.

'Dunno. Some slag in the sixth form.'

Both 'slag' and 'sixth form' made the Willy Sainsbury a dead cert. It wasn't fair. Kieron had been plotting skilfully to get somewhere with Ecstasy for weeks, and his own father swoops in and goes for the kill. And so *easily*. And he was *forty-eight*. As many years older than Ecstasy as she was older than Kieron. Why hadn't she thought twice about that? She hadn't thought his father too old, but she was sure to think Kieron too young. What had his Dad got, anyway? He was years past his prime and almost certainly couldn't get it up any more. That was probably why his mother had left. And why he hadn't kept all those girlfriends. Perhaps he should tell Ecstasy, or drop some sort of hint about the paternal impotency. But then maybe she'd think it ran in the family, and he would like to think they'd still be together when he was forty-eight. And she was ... Jesus, sixty-four. She'd be a young sixty-four, though. You could tell.

Before assembly Felix came out of the headmaster's office as Eve went in. She had been summoned for some reason and she was curious to know what it was.

He asked her how she was getting on and seemed pleased that she was settling in. He assured her that this was the only reason for asking to see her.

'Of course, we're not used to women teachers here. I'm glad that this hasn't presented any particular problems.'

There was a silence. He clasped his nose between his two index fingers and looked up at her.

'You aren't having any particular problems, I take it?'

She had half a mind to tell him about the phone calls. They could easily be from someone at school. But she didn't want to appear in need of special attention, being female.

'I don't think there are any problems,' she said, noticing that he was not looking at her and seemed awkward.

'Miss Swanbrook, you're a very ... attractive young...' The next word eluded him for a moment '...woman. Is there any reason,' he cleared his throat, 'why you're not married?'

She looked at the headmaster.

'No. I just haven't found the right person yet.' Pathetic.

'Well, at thirty-two, I suggest you think carefully. Women need to be fulfilled in that area. Children and so on.'

Eve had left feeling that someone had punched her full in the stomach. Any reason? Did he think you could select men off the shelves in Sainsbury's? Is that what he'd done? Was there any reason he *was* married, to that dreadful woman? Did he think she had tendencies? Was there any reason he'd asked her this question? She was confused. Adrian thought that was all she wanted and her employer thought that was all she should want. She went to W.H. Smith.

Eve loved stationers'. When she was down she would wander into Dowdswells or W.H. Smith and her heart would lighten at the potential of all that paper. While others bought themselves clothes, ate, smoked or drowned their sorrows in drink, Eve felt secure and stimulated among the address books, year planners, self-adhesive labels, hole-punchers, A4 and Copydex. Oh, the promise of narrow feint.

She had to handle it all, run her fingers along the bindings of diaries, try out the ball-point pens, open the tins. Always she would be tempted to buy a little something. Today it would be an eraser.

Primary Concerns

———— ◆ ————

After breakfast, Elvis came around the dormitories with the post. Kieron had already received a smutty card from Willy and a home-made one from Elvis. His mother had sent him a desk-lamp from Italy a few days before, and tonight he would have to see his father and pretend to have fun in a dreary restaurant. So long as he didn't take him to a pantomime or buy him lollies ... God, sixteen and no sign of a Sainsbury. Not even a Tesco.

Elvis knocked on Kieron's study door and handed him a postcard gloomily. 'It looks like one from your mother.'

Other people's postcards reminded Elvis that he wasn't getting any. And other people's mothers' postcards churned his stomach.

Kieron took it and put it on his desk, as though it were too hot to handle. Elvis went. Then, from a few feet away, he looked at it. The picture – of some Italian village – was small and set on a brilliant green background. Half of the card was taken up with giant yellow letters saying 'CIAO' with a fat red shiny heart, an exclamation mark, and 'Alberobello' written underneath. He watched it, as it seemed to him to move in front of him. The yellow letters were squirming slowly, as well they might, he thought. What would it say, this brief maternal note? He knew already. There would be lots of hugs and darlings and don't forgets. Don't forget to name-tag your socks and don't forget to write to Grandpa and don't forget to thank Mrs D for her present and don't forget to find out about Oxbridge *before* term ends and don't forget to go to your tennis coaching – it's a skill which will set you up for life, and it cost a small fortune. Don't forget. And don't forget me. Darling, darling, darling.

He sighed with exasperation, keeping dead cool before an invisible audience. Slowly he approached, flipped over the card, went to the window and read:

'Ciao, darling, x, You'd absolutely love it here – you must come and stay in Tuscany with us *soon*. We're back there next week – M says he'll teach you to surf – he's so FIT. Darling when can you come? – ask Pa. How's school? Can't wait to hear all your news, darling. Loads of hugs, Ma XXX.'

He turned the card over again. The red heart glistened fatly at him and the yellow 'CIAO' stopped squirming and screamed. He looked outside but the blue sky smirked back a disgusting primary blue. She couldn't say it to his face. She couldn't say it in black and white. She was saying it without thinking in screeching colours in sodding CIAO from Alberofuckingbello: *she didn't care if he forgot any more.*

He considered tearing it up dramatically, but it would have been a waste of high drama without an audience. He eyed Frizzle, his earless teddy, with a fleeting pang of guilt, in case he knew he didn't count any more. Anyhow, he wasn't certain enough yet to be so finally destructive. He wanted to believe he might have misinterpreted it.

'Good news?' Elvis popped his head round the door, hoping to absorb some maternal fall-out from the card, although he had already read it twice on the way down the corridor.

'*Ciao* off!' Kieron tore the card right through the red heart and threw the two pieces in the bin. Frizzle continued to gaze earlessly out at the blue sky, unimpressed. He immediately regretted it because he knew Elvis would have been grateful for even half a *Ciao*.

Cordelia

———◆———

Willy came in looking smug. Perhaps that was unfair and he just
looked very happy. Anyway, he seemed to have a permanent
smile on his face. Kieron was sitting back on his bed, waiting for
the dreaded inevitability of Willy's Sainsbury announcement. But
it didn't come. He was not going to give him the satisfaction of
quizzing him.

'I can fix you up too if you like, kiddo.'

'Oh yeah?'

'As a matter of fact, yes. Vicky's got a friend who really fancies
you. Hey, can you believe that?'

'As a matter of fact, yes.'

'Well then? Fancy a foursome?'

'Who is she?'

'Cordelia Francis.'

'Cordelia? She's in the sixth form.'

'Mmm. What d'you reckon?'

'The one with the long red hair? ... and ... well developed?'

Willy nodded.

Cordelia was tall, big-breasted, a sixth former, and terrifying,
but Willy had said she fancied him. What was she planning to
do, though? Would he be in control? Did it matter? Perhaps
Willy was having him on. But then, he wasn't getting anywhere
with Ecstasy since she'd chosen to have an affair with his Dad,
so why not?

'Fine.'

'Right then.'

'Right. Fine.'

At lunch-time Eve went to Sainsbury's to see if there were any men
on the shelves. She settled for Captain Birdseye Cod Fillets. Then
she returned to W.H. Smith for some solace. As she went through
the glass doors she spotted a couple standing by the magazines. He

had his arm around her shoulders and she was smiling down at him a lot. It was Kieron and Cordelia Francis.

Eve moved in a daze towards the sticky labels, and peered at the pair out of the corner of her eye. She was *taller* than him. And she was a *sixth* former. She was far too old for him. As Eve watched, the girl tossed her head so that her red hair fanned out and swung down her shoulders. They turned, and Eve bobbed back behind the display for cover. Cordelia Francis was very beautiful. And young.

Kevin

———❦———

Saturday night came round again and there was no word from Adrian. There was no one in detention either. Debbie had organised an outing to 'Bosco's' to cheer her friend up, but Eve was not looking forward to it.

Eve decided that she hated nightclubs only slightly less than she hated old boys' reunions, but she tried to look cheerful for Debbie. Young men stood around, thumbs hooked in jeans, hands pointed towards their genitals, glancing down occasionally to check. Young women were holding their stomachs in and smiling a lot. At first Eve had felt out of place. Towards the end of the evening she noticed very little.

'Hi. I'm Kevin, and you're...'

'Eve. Hey, I know you. You're a carrot.'

'Would you like to dance, Eve?'

'No thanks, Kev.'

'What are you drinking?'

'Oh ... I don't know, really,' Eve considered her glass vaguely and took a sip. 'Gin, I think – lots.'

'A pint of best and a double gin and tonic,' said Kevin, turning to the barmaid. Eve blinked, 'Thanks.'

The floor was beginning to pulsate. She decided gin was what she wanted. A lot of gin. She drank it quickly, grabbed her suitor by the waist and murmured, 'C'mon, let's dance.'

She placed one foot heavily somewhere in front of the other, and Kevin guided her to a corner of the dance floor where he acted as a prop for three slow numbers. Red and blue lights shot across the ceiling and yellow spangles slithered slowly over the walls. She swayed to the breathy beat of the songs, wrapped close to Kevin, who smelt decidedly Woody.

'Woody,' she said, looking up.

'What?'

Two cushiony lips came down on hers wetly, and when she

gasped for breath there was someone tapping her on the shoulder.

'Eve, this is Steve. He's going to take me home. Is that OK?'

Debbie was looking wearily radiant, her mascara smudged into two panda eyes and her nose glistening with sweat.

'Will you be all right, Eve?'

'She'll be fine,' said Kevin. 'I'll take her home.'

'I'll be f . . . f . . .'

'In fact, I'll take her now.'

Being Cool with Cordelia

It was ten o'clock and lights-out time. Kieron had sneaked into the girls' boarding house up the fire escape, and was sitting on Cordelia's bed. She had put some pulsating music on and was showing him her CD collection.

'Isı 't that a bit loud?' said Kieron, afraid of being discovered.

'So what? You're not afraid, are you?'

'Of course not.'

He lay back, dead cool, and looked at the photographs and posters that plastered her wall.

'Who's the man with the moustache?' he asked, trying not to look at his watch. The house tutor would be round soon. You never knew. They might just check up. Especially if there was music.

'That's James.'

'Who's James?'

'My bloke back home.'

'Oh.' Dead cool.

So Cordelia had a bloke back home. She wasn't his. She would never be just his. Kieron was indignant. It wasn't the thought of her being second-hand or anything. Ecstasy probably was too. But he didn't want to be an Also Ran. He wanted to be someone's man. To be important and powerful. The one person she dreamed of, sighed over at night when he wasn't there. The one man who could make her crumble into a heap and beg for him, for Kieron. He wanted to be unique to her.

She leant over him, her lips dangerously close to his, and said smiling:

'You're not jealous, are you?'

'Of course not.'

She pressed her large soft lips on his like a giant sea anemone, and he lay back under her pressure. She kissed and kissed him until he felt he had to unbutton her blouse. She heaved her large breasts across his pullover and he touched them carefully, trying to catch a glimpse of them. He wanted her, although he didn't care for her, but he might as well do whatever she wanted if she absolutely insisted like this. His heart was clumping riotously, half with excitement, half with fear at being caught. He closed his eyes and tried to think of Ecstasy.

Suddenly he heard footsteps in the corridor and doors slamming. He leapt up from the bed, pushing her aside, and ran to the window.

'God, you're so *boring*,' she was saying behind him as he disappeared down the fire escape.

Being Cool with Kevin

They had coffee. Kevin had made it while Eve protested her sobriety on the living-room sofa.

'Let's dance,' she said, now returning from the bathroom and hearing the music he had put on.

They clung together near the fireplace and swayed tenderly in the semi-lit room. She had had too much to drink, she knew. But only because she needed to relax. You had to live a bit. And anyway, she knew exactly what she was doing. She knew exactly what she was doing when she led him into the bedroom and pulled her dress over her head. She knew when he ran his hands over her suspenders and silk cami-knickers that she didn't want him to stop, that she wanted him to take them off very, very slowly.

He took them off very, very fast. The aching, the heartbeat, the soft, soft sheets. He would be gentle with her, he would know. The light from the yellow streetlamp spotlighting a few square feet of wall above them where nothing was happening; the curtains moving softly against the half-open window; his strong arms wrapping round her; the warm, damp fur of his underarms, the sweetness of his smell. Kieron. The hard legs entwining hers; the aching, aching, aching: two legs around two legs. The glorious symmetry of it all. The end of pain.

'Kieron,' she whispered.

'What?'

She moaned, breathed him in, bit at his salty shoulder. 'Oh, Kieron!'

'It's Kevin,' said Kevin.

She closed her eyes tightly in the darkness. 'Oh,' she groaned. And he could have sworn that in her ecstasy he had her sobbing.

At four a.m. Eve awoke to the dawn chorus and turned a bewildered face towards the neighbouring pillow. She pulled on a dressing gown and tugged at him.

'You have to go! You have to go!'

He awoke grumpily and, despite his slow protests, she made him dress. He went into the kitchen and she heard him closing the fridge door:

'Got any of that crunchy nut cereal, then?'

She pushed him out into the hall. 'Please, please go.'

He kissed her dryly and yawned as she shut the door on him. She leant against the door an instant, listening to the outer door open and close. Then she sank down on her haunches, screwed her face into a tight knot, and wept.

Threat

Later that Sunday morning the phone rang. Eve opened her eyes and saw the walls bright with sunlight and a gleaming pool of clothes by the bed. She switched the tape recorder on. It was Adrian. She switched it off again.

'Hi, Eve. What are you up to?'

Eve said nothing. She twisted a piece of hair around her finger. Adrian continued:

'You still there? I miss you, you know. I really do. And I've been thinking. You know all that stuff I said? Well, I don't really mean it. I was just frustrated that you never seem interested in what I'm doing – you don't support me in my career – do you know what I mean? Hey, are you still there?'

'Yes.'

'Anyway, I'm going to make it up to you. I'm taking you somewhere really special on Saturday, OK?'

'I've got cross-country.'

'Cross what? Well, can't you cancel it?'

Eve breathed out heavily. 'I can't. But I was going to ask ... You know the Downleaze ball I told you about? I bought two tickets weeks ago. I don't suppose you'd be my partner?'

'*Ball?* You're getting so bourgeois!'

'You wouldn't have to pay anything – I've already bought them.'

'You know I can't stand that sort of thing.'

'Shall I try and sell them back, then?'

'Whatever. Look, are you sure you can't cancel this thing on Saturday?'

'Yes.'

Then his doorbell rang and he had to go. 'Well, maybe I can take you out somewhere afterwards. It won't be the same, but I'll see what I can come up with. OK? Bye!'

The phone rang again and she left the receiver next to the tape recorder while she put on some clothes. After a few seconds she picked it up and listened.

'...we could meet up if you like ... I know you want me because you love listening to me, don't you? ... I know you're playing with yourself, aren't you?'

Eve felt the voice was familiar but was unable to put a face to it. It didn't sound like a boy's voice. It could be a boy with a deep voice, but no one she taught, or she would recognise it. It *could* be a member of staff, but who would want to...?

Suddenly she tried: 'I know who you are and I'm going to tell the police.' She hung up.

A moment later the phone rang again.

'You don't know who I am. But if you contact the police, you'll regret it. You wait and see.'

The Note

If it was a sunny day on Wednesday, Felix had promised, he would take a minibus down to the sea for those not in the teams. Thirteen boys from Pearce House had signed up to go and Eve had promised Felix, two weeks ago, that she would go too. She had forgotten to find a convenient excuse in the meantime. She would feel miserable sitting in the minibus facing Kieron for over an hour.

To Felix's surprise, she sat next to him in the front seat without any encouragement. He even rested his elbow on her knee during gear changes and she didn't hit him.

Kieron said nothing during the entire trip, but stared gloomily out of the window. His father was having an affair with his dream woman, and his first-ever girlfriend thought he was boring. He felt like ending it all, and pictured himself walking into the sea.

After about half an hour, the walking into the sea scene developed an interesting sub-plot. Miss Swanbrook saw him just as his head disappeared under a wave and, ripping her clothes off, swam out to save him. His head lolling between her naked breasts, she hauled him back to the shore, where she performed the kiss of life on him. She had been alone on the beach, so when he came to, they embraced, their naked bodies glistening in the sunlight. They were about to roll in the sand or make endless love in a convenient cave nearby, when the minibus came to a halt in a beach car-park.

They all scrambled out and Kieron ignored Eve when she looked at him. As they made their way down the shingle to the rocks, Kieron glanced at Eve, and she looked the other way, straight at Felix who smiled back and took her waist to guide her over the rocks. Bastard.

They reached a small beach hidden in the rocks. Behind it the cliffs rose up steeply and, to the other side, the rocks provided pools to explore and warm slabs to lie on. Miss Swanbrook sat on a large red towel and took out a sketchbook. Felix ran into the water heavily with the boys, and Elvis sat alone playing patience. Kieron tried to get him to swim, but he said he wanted to get brown. He stretched out his thin white limbs and smiled up at Kieron.

Half an hour later, Elvis ventured to the edge of the sea and let the waves slop at his feet.

'Come on, Elvis!' shouted Kieron. 'We're only playing ball – no racing or anything!'

'OK, in a minute,' said Elvis nervously.

'Now!'

Eve could see a look of panic on Elvis' face as three boys splashed towards him.

'Not just now,' she shouted. 'I'm trying to draw him.'

Elvis turned around and beamed. She drew him standing in the water, lying on his towel, and sitting playing cards. All he had to do was enjoy the sunshine, with no threat of physical activity.

Kieron was throwing a football high into the air, and watching Elvis. How was it he always managed to be the focus of Ecstasy's attention without the slightest effort? (He tackled Miles in the water.) Felix was getting out for a rest and went to sit on the towel with her. (He lost the ball to Duncan.) Felix was sitting very close and looking over her shoulder at the sketches. (He head-butted the ball.) It was time to get out.

He walked dripping across the shingle towards Elvis, dried himself with a towel and took out a notepad. He had been planning to write to his mother, but he wrote another note instead. He put the end of the pen on his chin and thought for a while. Ecstasy stopped drawing. Probably because it had entailed looking in his direction. Was he so revolting to her now? He wrote. He sealed the note in an envelope and handed it to Elvis.

'Here, Elvis. See this note? I want you to give it to Miss Swanbrook in five minutes' time, OK? *Exactly* five minutes. You got a watch?'

'Yes.'

'Exactly five minutes. OK?'

Elvis looked serious. 'OK.'

Kieron headed for the rocks, and Elvis watched the second hand on his watch. After four minutes he didn't see Miss Swanbrook go over the rocks back towards the car-park and the public toilet.

Suicide

As she made her way across a rocky cove, Eve noticed a figure wading into some rough waves. She recognised the nape of that neck. It was Kieron Oakey.

'Kieron! Kieron!'

He turned and looked.

'Kieron!'

He turned back and headed for the deep.

'Kieron, what are you doing?'

The water up to his armpits, Kieron turned round again, and shouted something.

'What?' strained Eve. The waves were crashing loudly and she couldn't make him out.

Why didn't she rescue him? She just stood there. With all her clothes on.

'I'm committing suicide!' he hurled.

Her face screwed up. 'I can't hear!' She cupped her hands. 'It's *dangerous*! Come back!'

'Oh, shit!' said Kieron, slicing the water with a karate chop. 'Shit! Shit! Shit!'

'*What*?'

Shit. This was typical. All he needed on the point of death was a deaf Samaritan.

Eve had returned to her towel and started to read when Elvis interrupted her.

'Excuse me, Miss Swanbrook, but Kieron asked me to give you this.'

She took the note and read:

Dear Miss Swanbrook,

I'm sorry it had to be this way, but I see nothing to look forward to, no hope for the future.

I would like you to have my entire CD collection and my sketchbooks (though Elvis can have 'The very Best of Elvis Presley' and 'Muddy Waters' and Willy can have all 'The Cure' and REM stuff). Also can you give Elvis my Levi 501s – he'll grow into them.

Please don't be upset. I'm sure you'll be very happy with my father and will find a way of telling him what has happened.

Kieron X.

How could he consider such a self-indulgent act? Didn't he have Cordelia to console him over his ridiculous false conclusion? She put the letter in her bag and saw Kieron clambering over the rocks towards the beach.

'Elvis, you didn't give me this note, OK? You lost it.'

'Right,' said Elvis, looking very conspiratorial, 'I lost it in the sea.'

Everyone was about to play water polo. They were picking teams, but Kieron did not want to take part. He had sat down on his towel, shivering, and Miss Swanbrook had not even looked at him. Elvis came over to tell him how she'd moved before five minutes was up and how he'd lost the note. Kieron was too miserable to be cross.

What Kieron needed was an excuse to rescue *her*. For that, he had to get her in the water somehow, out of her depth.

Kieron tried to persuade Elvis to commit suicide, but he wasn't at all keen. Elvis didn't want to say he couldn't swim. He had managed to avoid the swimming option for two terms and to produce notes about his sinus trouble all this term. He had come from a different prep school, so no one knew, not even Kieron.

The idea of putting an end to it all certainly had its appeal at the moment. But, thought Elvis, walking into the sea was not the ideal way to do it. It would be terrifying and it would play havoc with his sinuses.

Kieron was distraught. There had to be a way to attract her attention. He closed his eyes and within minutes had saved her from a passing shark. When he opened them again Elvis was prodding him, begging him to join one of the teams, or else there would be an odd number and he would have to play. Miss Swanbrook came to Elvis' rescue, asking him if he would help her fetch some icecreams. The two of them disappeared over the rocks.

'Come on, Oakey!' bellowed Felix, standing over him. 'If you won't play, I'll take your place.'

'Fine – I've hurt my leg anyway.'

He watched Felix bound down to the water's edge, the flesh rippling above his trunks. Then he turned and looked at the blank rocks over which had passed, barely a minute ago, the woman of all his fantasies.

Falling

Elvis was an easy boy to talk to. He was eager to be liked and put up no barriers to people around him. He bounded over the rocks looking into the deep blue water for jelly-fish.

'I used to dive off rocks like these – much higher than these – when my mother took me to Greece the year before last. Mother dives too.'

Eve sounded suitably impressed, but wondered why his mother wasn't Mum.

'Yeah. I used to dive twenty feet or so – about as high as that rock – then I'd go scuba-diving. I could show you if you like. You could see thousands and millions of fish and...' As he spoke, his foot slipped on the green slime of a sheer rock and he plopped into the water five feet beneath. Eve thought he had jumped in to demonstrate.

'You won't find any exotic fish in there, Elvis.'

But Elvis wasn't smiling. In fact, he didn't seem to see the funny side at all. His thin arms groped the air wildly and his eyes looked startled.

'I can't...' and his head bobbed under the water.

Christ! Eve slipped off her sandals and skirt and strode off the side of the rock clumsily. She tried to grab him but his arms flailed about, almost knocking her out. Eventually she clasped him around the chest and swam with him back to the shore.

She tried to pull him on to a low rock, but could barely clamber up herself.

'Bring him over here!' came a voice to one side. She looked up and saw Kieron, climbing down to the low rocks and signalling an easier way out of the water. He helped her lift Elvis – who was coughing like a seal – on to dry ground. She put him in a coma position and spread her cardigan over him.

It was then that she started shaking. She was pushing away a memory which tried to elbow its way into her head. She kept pushing it away, and it kept pummelling her until every limb shook. She could see Kieron. He was crouching there, worrying for his friend, stroking his head gently.

'It's OK, Trouble,' he was saying. 'Gold medal for diving, I think.'

He stood up, and looked at Eve. For an instant they just stood there on the rocks, looking at each other. She, struck by the beauty of his new-grown body, and he at the transparency of her wet underwear. Then he went towards her and put his towel around her trembling shoulders.

'You're shivering,' he said, and she smelt wafts of Kieron's warm skin and damp hair as he stood very close, his hands not leaving the towel around her shoulders. Musk, sandal, ambergris, myrrh: they flooded from Kieron as he spoke now, from the tone of his voice, from the buds of his tongue and the tufts of his hair. Along each arm she could see the taut muscles, and as he spoke she watched the lump in his throat glide up and down. His lips were so perfect, so close. She looked up into his eyes, and somewhere high up in the cliffs a camera clicked.

Neither of them heard it. Kieron had only now become fully aware of the wet skin inches from him, the quivering gold locket, the sodden white camisole top clinging to Ecstasy's breasts.

'Have my towel,' he said at last, releasing his hands. 'You'll catch your death of cold.'

Death to Cordelia

But it had happened. Kieron stared at the passing fields from the minibus. She had let him stand there, touching her. She hadn't moved to stop him. And she had looked into his eyes.

There were women who made you feel lonelier in their company than if you'd been all alone. It had been like that with Cordelia. It had been like that last time with his mother. All those smiles and darlings wrapped up in a huge parcel of nothing. And when they glistened and gleamed it was all for someone else, not for him. In Ecstasy's company he felt he was everywhere he ever wanted to be. He could have dialogues with her eyes. Her silence was more company than anyone else's words. When she smiled she threw him pearls, and when she spoke she filled an empty room with all the people he could ever want to hear. Her face was the secret land across a valley, and her eyes threw a bridge over to him. She was the end of sticker-books and loneliness. She didn't pull your hair or pinch your skin. She looked at you, and you knew she knew you.

Eve gazed at the road ahead as Felix brushed her elbow. She had been shaken. Kieron stood on the rocks putting the towel around her wet shoulders, time after time, all the way home. She wondered about Cordelia. By bed-time she was picturing her slipping off a rock, unnoticed.

Rumours

The headmaster had been nervous and excited all night. He had been unable to sleep, and had sweated a lot. In the morning his wife found him agitated, dropping some marmalade on the new white tablecloth.

'I've been tossing and turning all night, darling.'

'What's brought on the turning, dear?' asked his wife tartly.

And he explained what had been put on his desk the previous evening. She was equally appalled and excited. She drilled her husband on exactly what he should say that morning. She went over and over it, her eyes shining like rubies, so that when he arrived at his office he had a determined look in his face, and his palms were clammy.

Eve sat opposite the headmaster in horror. In front of her he held out a national tabloid paper with a large picture of herself and Kieron on the second page. 'SCHOOLBOY AND HIS MISTRESS REVEAL ALL' read the headlines. It went on to explain: 'Miss Eve Swanbrook and her sixteen-year-old pupil, Kieron Oakey, from Downleaze College, were caught with their trousers down yesterday when their secret love affair was snapped at Penkerris Bay...'

Her expression was rigid. The head was demanding an explanation.

'Headmaster, hasn't Felix Lamb told you about the accident? Surely you know that I dived in to save Elvis – Peter Ansell – from drowning? Oakey just came up with a towel for me afterwards. That was it.'

'I haven't spoken to Felix Lamb, no.' He began to sweat. 'But what I want to know, Miss Swanbrook, is why there should have been someone there to take the photograph. National tabloid photographers don't travel all that way unless they *think* they have a story.'

'Headmaster, I don't know who took the photograph, but I assure you there is no story. I've never touched Kieron Oakey.'

This could be tricky. He hadn't known about the trip to the seaside and he should have done. He had probably agreed to it some weeks back. He had had no idea about the accident or Felix Lamb's presence. His wife wanted nothing less than a dismissal and he desperately wanted to go to the lavatory. He would deal with it quickly. He had to stick to his guns.

'Well I've done some ... research. I've had the boy in recently about Saturday night detentions – five this term. He's never had any before on record. And who's taking Saturday night detentions? *You* are, Miss Swanbrook. You are.' He looked up, valiant. His toes felt very sticky in his socks. Eve was appalled.

'Headmaster, at the very worst, that might suggest that the boy likes me.' Her heart was thumping. 'Do we know who *took* the photograph? Was it a regular photographer?'

'What difference does it make? I see before me a semi-naked member of my staff with a semi-naked pupil of this school – a minor – in very close contact. Does it matter who *took* the picture?'

'Well, could it not be a prank? I mean, what if it were taken by a member of the school party? A lot of them had cameras, and it makes a very suggestive photograph – although the incident was totally innocent.'

The headmaster lined himself up with his Oxford freshman's picture above him. 'I wish I could believe you, Miss Swanbrook.' Gastric juices gurgled loudly around his toast and marmalade.

His suspiciousness was beginning to feel insulting. Suddenly Eve stopped being defensive and felt a surge of indignation. She had done nothing. She might have dreamt of all sorts of things, but she had done nothing.

'Headmaster, for the sake of my reputation and my career as a teacher, I think you should take very strong steps against this newspaper. You must interview Felix immediately and the members of the beach party. Everyone knew what happened. Everyone knew it could have been a very serious accident indeed.'

'Don't you think *this* is serious for our reputation as a top public school? We're in a recession as it is; this is all we need!' The head sounded angry, having no difficulty forming a sentence. Eve was furious.

'Not as serious as a child's death, Headmaster. No!'

She exited, pulled the door wildly behind her so that it whistled through the air like a cane, and then closed it gently.

Promising

* * *

After visiting the toilet, the head wandered out to Daphne for some solace. Flexing his hierarchical muscle he told her: 'That woman's days are numbered.' Daphne looked consoling, and added to her notepad list: *Dawn Haze Air Freshener*.

The headmaster had delayed confronting his wife as long as possible, but at ten-thirty he could find no more excuses for remaining in the office. When he arrived home he found a large scrawled note on the dining-room table:

Dear Wimp,
Your dinner is in the dog.

He crept upstairs to the bedroom, but the door was locked. He slunk back downstairs, opened a tin of Chunky Chicken, and ate it on his knee in front of the television. He watched 'Tarzan and the Mermaids' until one forty-five, when it ended, and he thought he heard his wife hammering on the ceiling. He switched channels, and watched the last hour of 'Star Trek' on full volume.

Watching the Dawn

It was one forty-five in the morning and the phone rang in Eve's flat.

'You haven't been behaving have you? I saw you with that schoolboy. I saw you all wet. I bet you couldn't wait to get him inside your...'

'You bastard! *You're* the one!'

There was a short silence.

'You don't know who I am. But if you tell anyone, *anyone* about our little conversations, I've enough evidence on you to make you very sorry. I know, you see. I know what you're really like.'

She was shaking. She phoned the police again. They told her it was probably some nutcase going through the phone directory and to hang up straight away next time.

It was one forty-five in the morning and Kieron couldn't sleep. He sat on the wide window-ledge of his study bedroom, hugging his knees and looking at the street below. Opposite was a great arch, gateway to Downleaze College. To one side of this, a boarding house, and to the other, playing fields. On this side of the road, Kieron could make out the front gardens of three boarding houses trailing up to the corner. Around that corner and out of view was the headmaster's palatial house.

Kieron had spent twenty minutes in the headmaster's office today. It had not been a pleasant experience. At first it had been quite exciting, seeing the picture of himself and Ecstasy, but then everything had seemed to turn very nasty. He had been interrogated like a suspect. He had come away feeling guilty and churned up.

The thought of everyone else asleep increased his feeling of isolation. All along the corridors of Pearce House, boys lay snoring gently in their bunks, nestled warmly in another world, clutching pillows, teddys or loins, pictures from page two of the offending

106

tabloid on their dormitory walls. Why did everything lovely have to be spoilt? Now he felt that if he even looked at her again he would be expelled. But he had done nothing. Nothing. Even now the adrenaline was on full alert, and his knees shook with cold and angst. The hedges below in the garden needed trimming, their leaves shining and flapping in the drizzle.

He heard the basement door open and shut, and Mr Avery's voice. Craning his neck, he saw a figure emerge from the side passage and then proceed up the garden path in full view of his window. It was a girl – a lower-sixth girl – Erica Rowan.

Kieron frowned and squinted as she closed the wrought-iron gate behind her and ran through the rain up to the girls' boarding house.

He was pondering on the significance of this event when a large, flashy car drew up opposite. The windows were dark and the wipers were still on. After five minutes the passenger door opened, and a woman stepped out on to the glistening pavement, covering her hair with a cardigan. She crossed the road towards him, and headed off around the corner. It was the headmaster's wife.

How silly to be dropped off so far from her own front door, especially in this rain. He felt a weak pang of pity for her, having to get into the same bed as the headmaster. Now she would be opening the front door; now she would be removing all her bits and pieces and woman's stuff in front of the mirror; now she would be taking off her clothes and putting on a nightie; now she would be rolling back the duvet and – poor sod – lying next to a sharp-nosed quasi-fascist who did all the things he was trying to accuse Kieron of. Pervert.

Following in the Footsteps

Saturday came round and Eve was aware that she was missing being taken 'somewhere special' by Adrian: he had still not forgiven her for being tied up with work. Twigs crunched under Eve's step as she walked through the local woods, map and felt-tip in hand. It was a bright damp morning and everything seemed to steam gently as the sun grew warmer. She rubbed her bright pink fingertips and breathed clouds into the cold air.

She had agreed to take on the cross-country this term, with no experience of setting trails, let alone running. It would be a one-off, she had been assured, just one house-run in the summer term and then no more until January and the regular Lent-term runs. All she had to do was set a sawdust trail beforehand and be there with a stop-watch at the end. Various past routes had been marked out on the map in thin red ink by Mr Culpin. Eve thought, with a start, that she was following in his footsteps, and hoped that wouldn't include the mysterious vanishing act at the end of term.

She had only a few yards to go now, and then she would rejoin her car at the end of the woods: the rest of the run would be track and road. She looked down: her feet were covered in leaves, mashed and browned, clinging like mud to her shoes. She stamped heavily along the road and scraped them along the lush grass on the verges. Suddenly, a rustling noise made her look back towards the woods. She could see nothing, and a raven flapping overhead reassured her. Then it came again and, turning, she thought she saw a figure, a dark shape, disappearing into the siding of the lane.

She started to walk briskly, passing a tractor, the sun emblazoning the windows into two opaque insect eyes. She ran now, reaching the car out of breath. She started driving, throwing great clumps of sawdust out of the windows.

Of course. Why hadn't he thought of it? It was so obvious that the headmaster's wife was having an affair, and Willy had spotted it straight away.

'Sometimes, you're a real Skoda.'

Kieron was tying the laces of his running shoes and feeling desperate.

'Yeah, I know, but I just couldn't imagine anyone *wanting* an affair with her.'

Willy sighed as he pulled on his shorts. 'It doesn't work like that, kiddo. One thing you've got to remember – they're all at it. God, even the headmaster does it – even the Queen – even Mr *Lamb* – everyone. And your Mum and Dad. Well, once anyway.'

Kieron looked up from his shoes.

'And your Mum and Dad.'

'And the prime minister.'

'And Cuthburtson!'

'That makes me feel a bit sick, actually. But – yip! Him too. Yuk!'

Willy was right, of course. But you had to admit, it was still hard imagining anyone turned on by Mrs Montague and her tight-lipped pomposity. Willy didn't find it difficult at all. He labelled all women and girls as 'women'. Partly because, if he was going out with one, it elevated his status to 'man'. But still, he made little distinction between any of them, except in terms of hair colour and breast size. Basically, women were objects of lust. They all thought the same, and provided the same service. Willy was unable to feel the erotic charge of a special glance, the uniqueness of one woman's expression, mood, eyes, smell, arms, nails ... Willy had no subtlety whatsoever. He was glad he hadn't considered the possibility of Mrs Montague's affair, even if Willy did think he was a dickhead. He didn't mind being a dickhead. He was sensitive, and probably would end up being a poet or artist or something.

'You'll probably be an accountant,' said Kieron, jogging out of the changing room a trifle smugly. Willy frowned at this non-sequitur. Sometimes he didn't understand his friend at all.

Minding

She spotted Avery in the distance and ran up.

'Hello, here's the child-molester,' he said, handing her a stopwatch and board. She frowned.

'Now, I want you to go back to the finishing line and get their *name* and *house* as they come in. Got that?'

'It's miles, and it's starting at two o'clock, isn't it?'

'You can cut across the woods.'

Eve had been walking for five minutes when it happened. The cracking of twigs behind her made her turn, but she saw no one. Then someone caught hold of her. She gasped.

'Hello there! I thought it was you,' said Felix breathlessly.

Eve looked at him, then closed her eyes and patted her heart in relief. He seemed excited, as if he had some news.

'You know, it's easy to get lost in these woods,' he puffed. 'Not safe for a lady on her own – especially a young attractive one like you.'

Eve lobbed him a sideways glance. He wondered if she had taken in his compliment.

'I expect all the men say that, don't they?'

Eve was crunching over the leaves at a terrific pace now, and he was looking at her breasts as he spoke.

'No,' she smiled limply. He seemed so pathetic and vulnerable that she didn't want to hurt him. He was walking just inches behind her now, desperate to breathe, desperate for love, lust or oxygen. She didn't want to deflate him, but she didn't want to encourage him either.

'I thought you might need some company,' he huffed, 'walking all on your own like this –' he puffed – 'a woman all on her own – and a very beautiful one ... We're not used to women doing this, you know.' (Huff.) 'Of course, you can't coach cricket, can you? I suppose they have to find *something* for you to do ... It's unusual

110

seeing you dressed up like that. You know, you ought to wear shorts – you'd look – ' (puff) – 'very good in shorts you would, you know.'

'I don't have any.' Eve was almost running.

'Not that these aren't nice,' he said, twanging the material of her tracksuit at her buttocks. She dodged her hips away from him. He panicked and clasped her elbow.

'There's no need to go so fast.' He swung her round.

She shook him off roughly.

'You don't mind me doing that, do you?' he said, clasping her buttock desperately, while the other hand shot up her T-shirt. (Quick! before she gets away – just one feel, quick – just one look!) She wriggled violently but he grabbed both wrists in his hands. You had to knee them in the groin. That's what it said in Cosmopolitan. But he pushed her against a tree and the weight of him trapped her. You had to poke their eyes out. That's what the ex-army officer had said at self-defence classes. He was grunting now. You had to knee them. You had to scream. Of course. She bellowed and a hand clamped over her mouth, the edge of it seeming to block off both nostrils too, so that she felt her face would burst with lack of air. She could see the red skin of his face shining and the tufts of his remaining mud-coloured hair, flat and sweat-soaked against his temples. You only had to keep your legs crossed and gouge their eyes out and everyone knew nothing could happen if you really didn't want it to. He was tugging at her tracksuit. And the worst crime was letting yourself get into the situation in the first place.

'I don't want to hurt you,' he was saying, fumbling one-handed. (Almost there! And she would love it, he knew. As soon as he got there she would stop all this nonsense and just melt.) But the quest for the breast required two hands, and in his examination he forgot that the wrists and mouth were free. She shoved him with such force and with such a cracking scream that he teetered backwards and almost fell. She ran.

He ran a few paces after her, and stood bewildered, calling: 'I didn't think you'd mind! ... Eve! ... I didn't think you'd *mind!*'

Ecstasy in the Woods

The race had been on for twenty minutes and Miles, Willy and Kieron formed a cluster running abreast as they entered the woods.

'You know who's time-keeping, don't you?' said Miles knowingly.

'Yeah. Her and ten other people,' said Kieron, with a fairly successful attempt at nonchalance.

'We'll have to watch you don't dash off into the woods for a quickie,' laughed Miles, not giving up.

'No probs,' said Willy, panting heavily, 'he wouldn't know what to do!'

'Fuck off, Willy!' Kieron edged ahead down the narrow track.

'Oh, *lordie*,' said Willy, smiling at Miles, '*what* a little tantrum.'

They ran in silence for a while, in and out of the flickering sunlight.

'Hey, Kieron,' said Willy at last, 'don't get so screwed up over her. There's plenty more fish in the sea.'

That was typical of Willy. 'She's different.'

'Look, Kieron. What's worse, being without one woman who doesn't have much promise anyway when there are billions of potential Sainsburys out there, or getting kicked out for a quick peck on a Safeway cheek?'

Miles looked confused at all this talk of shops. He was about to ask for an explanation when he saw Miss Swanbrook herself, running out of the woods on to the wide path ahead.

'Look!'

They all looked up and saw her run straight into the arms of Mr Avery. She buried her head in his armpit and stayed like it. Willy increased his speed to look, but Avery led her off the path. They passed the couple, heads turning in unison to get a closer look at the details.

Willy was running backwards now, ahead of the other two.

'Well bugger me sideways! Who would've thought...? She

doesn't let the grass grow under her feet, kiddo, I'll say that for her. He's got his arms round her now. He's stroking her head. Look! He's...'

'Shut it, Willy!' said Kieron. 'We don't want to know.'

He really didn't want to know at all. Not interested. Nope. Not at all.

Someone called Joshua Mead-Byrne came in first, followed by Angus McClaughlan, a fourth former. Kieron, Miles and Willy were somewhere towards the end, trailed only by a couple of emaciated third formers. Mr Avery singled the three boys out as everyone was getting in the coaches to go back.

'You three – pathetic! You're all capable of better than that!'

'Except me, sir,' said Willy.

'Except you, Page,' conceded Avery tersely. 'I want you all to cut back through the woods via the shortest route and look for Miss Swanbrook's stop-watch. If you're not back at the start in fifteen minutes *with* the watch, we'll go without you. OK?' and he signalled to the driver to start up.

High up in the hills were some fields belonging to Downleaze College and, skirting them, Shepherd's Woods. Wide paths crossed the woods from road to road, and smaller paths meandered from field to field. But only one tiny path led a straight route through the woods from Downleaze College fields to the finishing post of the annual run. Along this narrow, overgrown path Kieron and his friends walked, bent double, scouring the leaves like sniffer dogs. Willy took the path itself, Kieron walked to the left, and Miles to the right.

Kieron's back was beginning to ache, and his face and arms were assaulted by protruding twigs. It was all very strange. First a lesbian lover, then his father, and now Mr Avery. But there had definitely been something between her and Kieron, hadn't there? Even the newspaper picked up on that. He was determined to find the stop-watch, because he had an idea. If he found it, he wouldn't tell the others. He would slip it in his pocket and use it as an excuse to go and see Ecstasy. Then he would find out what was going on. I'm sorry to bother you, Miss Swanbrook, but I found this in the woods, and I believe it's yours. How kind! Do come in and have a cup of tea. Thanks. Sugar? Milk? Biscuit? Now I come to think of it, I've just made a chocolate cake, if you'd like some. Mmm. My favourite, actually.

'Found it!' shouted Miles, waving a clipboard. 'It must be near this – there!' and he gave the board to Kieron as he picked up the red plastic stop-watch.

Kieron felt miserable. They jogged back towards the college fields where the three blue-painted 1960s buses were waiting to take them back to school. Perhaps he could do a deal with his friends? But then they'd all have to walk home and it was miles. They'd definitely refuse.

As they reached the buses, Kieron slipped the red felt-tip pen at the top of the clipboard into his pocket.

Back at school they showered, dressed, and sped off to the tea queue. Kieron slipped away in the rush and went back to his room.

He dabbed aftershave under his arms and rinsed his mouth out with toothpaste. He put on his best pullover, and then took it off again. Best be casual.

He ran down the stairs, strolled out on to the pavement, and walked briskly down the three streets to the top of Miss Swanbrook's road. He stood on the corner, rehearsing his lines gently into the hedge. He applied some lipsalve and practised a smouldering look. Then he made his way to the front door.

In the Bag

When Eve arrived home she showered, and then she showered again. The phone rang and she ran to the bedroom, poking her arms into a red dressing gown, and stood looking at the trilling object. Then she picked up the receiver.

'Hello? Eve?'

'Adrian!'

'Hey listen. You're not going to believe this, but I can't make tonight. There's this chap – Anthony Carding – and he's like God in academic publishing – loads of influence and all that. Well, he's challenged me to a game of squash *tonight*, can you believe that?'

'Yes.'

'So I can't refuse. I mean, you can't turn down that sort of thing, and you did say you had sport or something, didn't you? So it all works quite well. But look, I'm not going back on my promise – I'll take you out tomorrow. And that's a promise. You might even twist my arm to go to that dreadful ball.'

'Adrian, I've got to talk to you.'

'That's OK. Eight tomorrow?'

'No. You don't understand. I need to talk to you now. Could you come round? I've been...'

'Pretty down, huh? Well, me too, actually. The thing is, Mum's here at the moment. I can't just leave her – she's been doing all my washing and ironing.'

Sigh. 'Can I come round? It's really important.'

'She's just in the middle of cooking me something.'

'Why can't...?'

'Look, don't start that again. She *likes* doing it. It gives her something to do. She gets real pleasure from ironing my shirts...'

Eve held the receiver away from her and looked at it. She placed it back on the telephone gently.

She heard Debbie's footsteps on the stairs and went to her front door.

'Debbie!'

'Eve! You look awful!' She was clomping down the last few stairs and was heading for the front door.

'Debbie, can I talk to you?'

'Of course. I've just got to take the rubbish out – you've forgotten too.' She went into Eve's kitchen and picked up her bin-liner. 'The dustbin men are down the street – I must catch them. Hang on!' She came up to Eve and put her hand on her arm: 'Hey, Evie, I'll be right back. Don't you go worrying, now!' She opened the outside door and turned back: 'Put a paper bag over your head or something!'

Eve went into her living room and sat on the sofa. She held her knees and rocked backwards and forwards. Her face was tense and painful, and tears stung on her cheeks. A knock on the door of her flat heralded Debbie. She grabbed a W.H. Smith bag and went to the door.

To Kieron's surprise, the front door was ajar. He hovered by the doorbells, and then decided to step inside.

The door was opened by a woman with a bag over her head.

'I'm sorry,' said the bag. 'Something awful's happened.'

Kieron stood very still and looked at Miss Swanbrook. It was her voice, but there was a tearful note in it which he hadn't heard before.

'Hello, it's me.'

'Kieron!' Her hands went up to remove the bag, but then stopped. 'I'm sorry ... I'm sorry – I look terrible.'

There was something very wrong. Kieron could hear her loud, jagged breaths, and hoped he hadn't frightened her. He put out his hands and gently removed the bag.

She looked at Kieron, and swallowed. He stood looking at the wet, pink face, and then said: 'I brought back your felt-tip pen – I thought you might need it.' He held it out.

She nodded a lot, 'Thanks,' and smiled. 'I've missed it.' Then she bit her lip, and her hands went up to cover her face again. Kieron sat down awkwardly on the arm of the sofa.

Miss Swanbrook didn't look anything like the women you saw crying in films. Her eyes were as red as a hamster's and had shrunk into two small slits. Her face was purple-red and blotchy. She was looking down at her knees, clasping them, and plucking at bits of thread in her dressing gown. Her expression had fixed into a stiff grimace – almost like a smile – and he could tell from her lack of

116

breath that it was repressing a painful explosion of sobs. Then two tears spilt over from her eyes and sped down her face. He moved over to her and put an arm around her shoulders.

'Don't cry,' he said gently.

This had the effect of sending Miss Swanbrook into a tirade of sobs.

'I'm sorry,' she whispered.

He wondered if he could stroke her hair, or if that would make her recoil. He could feel her shoulder trembling.

'What's the matter?'

She breathed very deeply and looked at the floor.

'Something awful's happened.'

'I know about the newspaper article. Please don't be upset. When I find out who took that picture...'

'No, it's not that. It's worse.'

Kieron felt panic. 'Have you been given the sack?'

'No!' she almost chuckled. 'No, I've ... no, not that. Maybe I'm overreacting.'

'What? What is it?'

She was fiddling with the tie of her dressing gown and didn't look up.

'I've been ... attacked. Well ... yes. Today – in the woods ... But it's not that, it's *everything*...' and she was crying again. Kieron tightened his arm around her shoulders, and she sank her face into his chest, so that he could feel the tight muscles of her expression.

'Bastard! I'll kill him!' Who on earth could...? Did she mean she'd been...?

She clung to him now and, without really thinking, he kissed the wet hair on the top of her buried head. She looked up. He smelt the salty tear-tracks on her cheeks and saw the swollen lips, just inches from his own. He tilted his head, forgot to look smouldering, and approached slowly...

'Coo-ee!' A key was tapped sharply on the flat's open door. 'Never fear, Debbie's here! ... Oh!'

Debbie stood at the living-room door. Kieron jumped up from the unconsummated embrace.

'I was just going,' he said.

It was the woman from the bed.

Sex

As they lay in bed the following day, Eve and Adrian looked into each other's eyes. She was thinking about Felix. He looked back and thought about a Milky Way he had put in the fridge to eat later.

'Women just don't understand men's need for sex,' Adrian had said to her once when he was feeling particularly critical of her performance in bed.

Eating pasta made her think of sex because of Italians; eating salad made her think of sex because of rabbits; dogs made her think of sex because they sniffed private parts; cats made her think of sex because that's all they thought of; flowers made her think of sex because of the stamens; grass made her think of sex because you could do it on it; trees made her think of sex (for some reason); car toll-gates made her think of sex because they rose up stiffly; men's voices made her think of sex because they were deep; school chapel made her think of sex because it repressed it; trousers made her think of sex because they concealed it; libraries made her think of sex because you could exchange erotic glances in them; television made her think of sex because there was always plenty of it on it; sun made her think of sex because it was hot; rain made her think of sex because it was wet; buttons made her think of sex because they sounded like buttocks; sweat made her think of sex because it was produced during it; hands made her think of sex because of the fingers; shoes made her think of sex because of the tongues; gossip made her think of sex because it sounded like gusset; bikes made her think about sex because of the helmets; walls made her think about sex because you could do it up against them; bells made her think about sex because they vibrated; hymn-books made her think about sex because they told you not to; rules made her think about sex because they were rigid; God made her think about sex because it was heavenly; Adam's apples made her think about sex because they protruded; eyes made her think about sex because some knew what you were thinking; tables made her think about

118

sex because you could bend over them; games made her think about sex because of the balls; keyboards made her think about sex because of the fingering; music made her think about sex because of the heartbeat; toothpaste made her think about sex because of the squirting; hair mousse made her think about sex because of the pump action; soap made her think about sex because it was slithery; bald men made her think about sex because of their testosterone; carpet made her think about sex because of the shag pile; socks made her think about sex because they sounded like sex; and queuing made her think about sex because you had to think about something.

Perhaps the best sex she'd had since knowing Adrian had been standing up against the washing machine on a fast spin. Adrian had been in the living room doing a spreadsheet on famine.

Talking

On Monday he watched her come out of the refectory and head towards her teaching room. He followed swiftly, knowing he could catch her alone before lessons started.

She was sitting at her desk (looking wistful, he thought).

'Hello,' said Kieron.

She looked up, startled. (Surely she'd been expecting him.)

'I was just passing.'

'What can I do for you?'

(Rip my clothes off, lay me on the desk-tops, stroke me kiss me suck me all over. Smother me with your naked body; be my Sainsbury...)

'I brought you this.'

He placed a small object on her desk wrapped in green tissue paper. 'It's nothing – I thought it might be useful for the Art room.'

Eve unwrapped it, and found a small model elephant the size of an egg.

'I only wrapped it because ... you know ... I had some paper. I just thought people could draw it, maybe ... or something...'

Eve put her chin down on the desk to look across at the elephant closely. She smiled.

'It's beautiful. Thank you.'

'There's something else for you – it's in my sketchbook. Don't look at it now.'

Eve began to look uncomfortable. 'You mustn't keep giving me things.'

'It's nothing. Look...'

Eve started to wrap the elephant in its tissue paper.

'We've got to talk,' he said (manfully).

There was a silence.

'What about?'

'You know – about what's happened.'

'And what's that?'

'You know – being attacked and everything.'

'I don't think we have to talk.'

'But you *must* report it.'

'Why?'

'Because if you don't, he'll do it again.'

'No one would believe me.'

'You've got to try.'

'I've no evidence.'

'That's no reason.'

'Under the circumstances – what with all this newspaper stuff – I'd just become even more an object of ridicule.'

'Perhaps that's why it happened.'

'You don't understand, Kieron. You can't just...'

'"You don't understand, Kieron"! Yes I bloody well do understand. And if you don't report it, then I will.'

'Kieron, don't be ridiculous.'

'It's irresponsible if you don't.'

'There's more to it – it's someone ... we know.'

'Tell me who it is – I'll kill him! Who is it?'

'It doesn't matter.'

'Who is it?'

'You'd better go.'

'Ecstasy, who is it?'

'What did you call me?'

'Nothing.'

There was a graceless silence.

'You'd better go, Kieron.'

He sat limpet-like on the edge of the desk. 'I'm playing in a concert next Monday. Are you coming?'

'Kieron! You mustn't be seen with me alone like this. Don't you understand? We're in enough trouble already. *Please* try to help me!'

'But that's why we need to talk.'

'No we don't.'

'We do!'

'What about?'

'You and me.'

'No we don't.'

'We do.'

'Go.'

'No.'

'Kieron, go!'

Elvis poked his head around the door.

'Go, Elvis!' said Kieron.

'No, stay – Elvis, come here.'

Elvis stood in the doorway and looked at Kieron. 'I've got Art now,' he said limply.

'Sod off! You're early.'

'Elvis, come in.'

Kieron flared his nostrils and went.

Love Lost

After lessons, Eve opened Kieron's sketchbook and found dozens of rose-petals. She went to sit under the magnolia tree, looked across the field and contemplated the strange patterns of her love-life.

Teddy Bowan had been seven when Eve met him, and she had been eight. He told her his elder brother was a famous boxer and his mother was an actress in Hollywood. She believed everything he said until her parents told her he came from the childrens' home and had no family. But she loved him even more, and liked to listen to stories about Graham the boxer and where he was fighting next. She wanted to share her parents with him, and so she invited him home to tea. He wouldn't come, so she said it was her birthday and her mum was preparing a special tea. She said her mum had insisted he was more than welcome; in fact, she would be disappointed if he didn't come.

There was no jelly. There was beans on toast. No ice cream and chocolate cake, but some leathery jam in the bottom of a jar. Her mother was cross at the lack of notice because the tablecloth needed washing. Teddy was awkward. He gave Eve his Action Man wrapped up in a W.H. Smith bag because he had no money to buy her a present. Eve cried because it wasn't her birthday, and because her Mum told them to clear off and play in the garden.

When Teddy was fifteen he drowned during a day-trip to Dawlish.

A large petal flopped noiselessly on to her lap. She looked up and saw that the magnolias were wide open, petals drooping but turned up at the tips like elegant chandeliers. At any other time she would have wanted to paint them, but all she could do was look up at their simplicity, their ready abandon to the summer.

Her first exhibited painting had been when she was five years old. Donald Duck in the local Art gallery. She had been knee-high and there were paintings everywhere you looked. Too many and too high. Fruit, army tanks, flowers, guns, butterflies, faces, serpents, boats and bodies. She gazed up for a long time at the whole effect, unable to see any detail, and holding on to her father's leg so as not to keel over in her dizziness or lose him in the crowd. She concentrated on the shoes, the hems of coats and small dogs low enough to establish eye-contact with. She clung on tightly and let her head loll back to catch the span of the ceiling, cracked and peeling above the powder-painted glory. The horror when she saw it stayed with her now. A strange feeling of betrayal, of loss, of panic. He towered above her, this man whose knee she clasped for security. He looked indifferently at the paintings. *But it wasn't him*. It was some other man, some stranger posing as her father. She let her arms drop from the treacherous thigh and stood, mouth open and alone. The owner of the leg looked down, relieved, and sidled away. She looked around. There were plenty of legs, but only one pair that smelt of home.

Adrian wasn't just Adrian. He was the scores of treacherous shoes upon the mat. He was Roger who'd left her to walk home alone and made love to her best friend; he was David who'd run down her paintings and flirted with other women when she sold any; he was Brian who'd sent up her ambitions at dinner parties; he was Douglas who said she'd be top of his list if she lost a few pounds when he found out she had an M.Litt.; he was Stephan who claimed all other women came within sixty seconds; he was Patrick who made love with his trousers on and complained that her slippers depressed his libido; he was Tom who called women 'tarts'; he was Charlie who smelt of sock and wanted women with no leg or underarm hair; he was Alex who'd packed her in for a check-out girl when she hadn't noticed his car was a posh one; Adrian who'd banged on the wall to tell her neighbours to be quiet.

And the feelings she had for Kieron were so filled with tenderness and shame. A shame she had misunderstood, for Kieron was not just Kieron. He was Paul who'd tried to sit next to her at primary school; he was the boy at the end of the road who'd sent her unrequited Valentine cards for five years; he was Richard who'd walked her home and given her his pullover to keep warm; he was Peter who'd kept some strands of hair from her hairbrush in his encyclopedia; he was Andrew who'd tried to turn a peck into a kiss for years; he was Frank who'd called round with Lem-sip when she was ill; he was Bernie who she discovered had bought all the paintings sold at her first exhibition; he was Colin who'd written 'please let me love you' on every sheet of toilet paper in her bathroom; Daniel whom she'd left standing at a bus station, saying she could never love him. Love running arms outstretched. Love left standing on platforms and pavements.

The Kiss

Well, she needed some plants for the Art room, something new to draw from the immense grounds filled with flagrant summer. And was it maybe a little deliberate that she chose the front field, knowing his room overlooked it? Did she maybe hope to come across him, see him from afar, locate him in the order of things on that hot slow evening? Nothing conscious formed itself, but as she went out with her basket and summer dress she felt like the brazen evening blooms.

There was a corner of the field where the roses were more abandoned and unpruned. It was here, where the mown grass met the lush uncut grass, that the field descended into an untamed tangle of meadowsweet, cornmint, willowherb and bindweed. It was to this corner that Eve found herself moving in search of the bushiest clusters of unplucked roses. Kieron watched from afar, his lips freshly salved. There she stood amongst the pink and the white and the peach roses, blooming thickly. She snipped the stems with her secateurs and pulled them out rustling from the leafy tangles, placing them in the growing, blooming bunch in her basket. Hovering over one, she stroked its velvet petals and pressed it to her nose and cheeks. She sneezed violently. And as she turned her cheek, she saw him, like a fox stealthily approached. Where once there was a space, now was he; eyes gleaming into her, cheek glowing.

She took the rose away swiftly. 'Hi.'

'Hello. You picking those for your flat?'

'No. For class.'

'I saw you – I was just passing – walking – taking a stroll – I thought you might like a hand.'

'Oh, I'm OK, thanks.'

'You've scratched your hand.'

The speedily dropped rose had written a thin red line along her arm. He touched it, pointing at it in the softness of her limb. She withdrew it, looking at the basket on the ground.

'You could help with...'

...and he touched her mouth.

'You've got some pollen...' and he brushed away the pollen with his thumb. And he brushed her lips and lingered fearlessly over the contours, standing very close. The roses were shedding their scent in a heady rampant explosion of smell. She saw his lips close to hers, like a glistening, luscious fruit. He bent forwards, very deliberately, and kissed her softly and shamelessly on the mouth.

It was a long, torrid, gentle, warm, fluttering kiss, full of the saps and scents of growing, sprouting, succulent summer. She smelt his warm skin amongst the rocketing frenzy of wanton summer smells. She told him to go, and he went.

Looking

It was about that time that the eye-contact began. Never before had looking been so electric to either of them. They looked searchingly in assembly, seeking the other's presence and acknowledgement: they looked furtively in study lessons, glimpsing each other for an instant over the pages of novels: they looked wistfully, caressing the contours of the unaware face: they looked earnestly, fearing a change in the affectionate map explored the day before; they looked dangerously, meeting the eyes and jabbing shamelessly at the senses: they looked intrepidly, holding the gaze steadily for long seconds, tunnelling deep behind the irises until there was no turning back. They had discovered a magic that wasn't taboo, and they looked and stared and gazed ravenously, as if they had uncovered a new sense.

Left Standing

Eve sat at her desk and thought. She was thinking about him far too much, she thought. She saw those lips approaching her – everywhere. She saw him kissing her saltily by the sea with crashing waves, kissing her hotly on warm rocks, kissing her wetly on hot sand, kissing her furtively in the bookroom, kissing her tenderly under the arches, kissing her wickedly in the chapel pews, kissing her impetuously on the stairs to her room, kissing her feverishly against the blackboard, kissing her again in the field by the roses, and again and again and on the neck and on the breasts and again and again and all over...

There was a knock at the classroom door. She didn't answer. Kieron pushed open the door and came in.

'We've got to talk.'

'Not again.'

'We didn't talk last time.'

'I think we did.'

'Things were different last time.'

There was a silence. She saw his glorious lips and looked away.

'Kieron, you and I must never be alone again. Do you understand?'

'Why not?'

'Because...'

She looked at him. That dear, impish face had grown up suddenly. It looked at her with reasoned determination.

'I *must* see you.'

'We mustn't be alone together. Anyone could walk in.'

'Anyone *won't*.'

'They might.'

'Let them.'

'Look ... what happened ... it must *never* happen again.'

'Why not?'

'I could lose my job! Kieron, this is deadly serious. If we were seen, I'd lose my job just like that – if I haven't already.'

'You don't like it here anyway, do you?'

'I'd lose my job *and* never get another one!'

Silence.

'And you'd be expelled.'

'That's a risk I'm prepared to take.'

More silence. She breathed out heavily. He gave her a piercing stare.

'We can't deny what's happening to us.'

She stifled a smile. Did he think this was a black-and-white movie?

'We can and we will!'

'So you admit there is something happening.'

'No!'

'You can't deny it.'

She covered her face with her hand and sighed, *'Kieron!'*

He settled himself on the edge of a desk. 'Do you think it's possible for a teacher to have a relationship with a pupil?'

'Which teacher and which pupil did you have in mind, I wonder?'

'You, of course – and me.'

'No.'

'Why not?'

'I've told you!'

'Is that the only reason?'

'Look, you're fifteen – you're a minor...'

'I'm *sixteen* – I'm legal now.'

'Legal for what?'

He poked at a piece of loose Formica on the desk.

'I'm twice your age.'

'I don't care!'

'What do you mean, you don't care?'

'Look...'

'I'm not looking for a fling – I can have flings with anyone – without...'

'You're looking for something more enduring.'

'How do you know?'

'I do.' He looked directly at her. 'And I can give you that.'

'I'm old enough to be your mother.'

'I don't care! It *can* work. My uncle's twenty years older than his new woman, and they're getting married.'

'Well, he's a man!'

'God! Stop being so sexist!'

'Stop being so mature!'

He looked all trilby and trenchcoat again.

'I'm not going to give up.'

'Go now.'

'No.'

'Well, *I'm* going.'

She picked up her keys and went to the door. He followed her down the corridor, down the stairs, out on to the pavement and up to her car.

'I'm not just a poxy sixteen-year-old, you know.'

She got into her car and rolled the window down.

'Kieron, please don't be seen with me like this.'

'I don't think you realise what my feelings are for you,' he was saying as she rolled the window up. She started the engine and he pressed his face to the window.

'I love you!' she saw his lips shout through the glass, and she drove away, leaving him standing in the road.

No Sweat

———◆———

On Sunday Kieron took his bike out and went cycling round in a loop which passed her flat. At midday he saw her get into her car and drive off. She hadn't seen him so he followed.

After a while he saw her car disappear behind the leaves of a country lane, and he knew he could catch up with her easily on the slow curves of the road. Ten minutes later he was still cycling, and still he couldn't see her. The sun was directly overhead and the low hedgerows offered no protection. He was sweating and annoyed for not having thought about sweat. Sweat would ruin any meeting with her anyway. Then he saw the bonnet of her car at the side of the road. He dismounted and rummaged for a handkerchief. Realising he never kept handkerchiefs, he swore to himself and kicked the bike. Quickly, he shed his shirt and T-shirt. He wiped his face with the off-white T-shirt and sighed. Then he sniffed his underarms and groaned. They nearly knocked him out (what would they do to her?). He rubbed them vigorously with the T-shirt which he then tied roughly to the handlebars. Then he replaced his shirt, applied some lipsalve, and took a deep breath.

She wasn't in the car but, peering over the adjacent gate Kieron saw her at a distance, sitting under a tree. He took his bike twenty yards back down the lane and started to cycle past the gate as if he had never stopped.

'Hi!' he shouted, turning his head casually as he reached the clearing. But she didn't hear him.

If he walked over to her she would think he'd followed her, not seeing the pure coincidence of his passing. He took the bike back down the lane and repeated the manoeuvre.

'Hi! Hi there!'

Still no response. He couldn't do it again. What if she'd seen him and chosen to ignore him? He decided to take the bike with him, so he opened the gate and pedalled across the uneven long grass in her direction. Given the failure of Plan A, there was now a pressing need to appear casual. He took his hands off the handlebars and placed them on his thighs. No sooner had he done this than he realised his gamble. The ground rose and fell at random and grassy clumps were interspersed with cow-pats. He fell, sweating and manured, at her feet.

'You're always falling off bikes,' she laughed, paintbrush in hand. Beside her was an open box of water-colours. If she was surprised to see him, she didn't show it, which made him feel comfortable. He sat down beside her and she smiled, as if it were quite natural that he should.

'Help!' she said suddenly. 'My sky's running – quick, where's the sponge?'

She looked around for something to mop up the grey of the sky, and alighted on the T-shirt a few inches away from her on the handlebars.

'Oh, I'm really sorry! I've ruined your vest.'

'No! No! It's fine – I don't want it any more. It's just an old rag – honestly – use it.'

He watched as the Payne's Grey, which had spidered into the grain of the water-colour paper, was stopped dead in its track by his underarm sweat.

'So what are you doing here?' she asked.

'Oh, I was just passing. I saw your car and I thought: I know that car...' It was useless to give long explanations. They would only betray premeditation. Easy does it. No sweat.

'Well, now you're here, entertain me.'

'Have you got a spoon?'

'A spoon?'

'I can hang a spoon on my nose.'

'No, nothing visual. It'll put me off. Talk to me – or sing – can you sing?'

Kieron couldn't. Why hadn't he taken singing lessons when his father had insisted? Then he could impress her and she'd be completely bowled over. She'd look at him, Kieron, all deep-voiced and manful, and drop her water-colour brush into the grass. Her pretty mouth would fall open while her sky ran in wild rivulets. Then he remembered he hadn't taken singing lessons *because* his father had insisted.

He told her a limerick, and she told him one. Then they made some up. They were laughing and he forgot all about sweating and not being able to sing. She gave him some paper and showed him how to do a wash for the sky. Soon he was telling her about everything: his father, his mother, Cuthburtson's punishments, Elvis.

And what would they say, Cuthburtson or his father or his mother's lover, if they could see him now? What would they say if they could see him sitting with her, his elbow brushing her warm arm as they laughed? He lined up all the people he wanted to annihilate, made them stand in awe for a moment and watch him easy in the smiley shade with Ecstasy, then he clicked his fingers and they were all trampled underfoot by the herd of bullocks in the neighbouring field. He could hear the thunder of their hooves. He could hear the pounding, pounding, pounding...

'What's that?' said Ecstasy, listening.

'What?'

'That music?'

It was Kieron's Walkman on his bicycle.

'Mascagni – *Cavelleria Rusticana*,' he said, turning it up as loud as it would go.

'It's beautiful.'

'I'm supposed to be playing it next week,' he said.

'What do you play?'

'Violin.'

She was impressed. The music stopped, then restarted.

'And this is Strauss.'

He mimicked playing Strauss on his violin.

'Can you waltz?' she asked.

'No.'

'*What*?'

Pathetic. He felt hopeless. Then she got to her feet:

'I'll show you – you've got to know how to waltz.'

She tugged at his clammy hand. He resisted, but only because he wanted her to hold his hand some more. They almost fell over in the struggle to make him stand.

'One two three, one two three – like this – it's easy.'

They stepped between the thistles and the cow-pats, one two three amongst the clover. Soon they were whirring round and the horizon seemed to spin them into a ball of laughter. Then the music stopped. He thought how easy it would be to fall over in their dizziness. Just one small trip and he could bring her down on to the soft grass. But it would spoil everything.

She was walking back to the tree when *Elvira Madigan* began. He went and stood next to her.

'Stop!' he said. 'Listen to this.'

He hummed to it. She smiled.

'Listen – it's beautiful!'

She had her back to the tree, and he could smell the bark. He put one hand against it, half enclosing her. He was aware that his armpits reeked of sweat, but he didn't care. Her nose was about six inches from his and he was probably breathing the same air. He looked at her eyes and they seemed afloat.

'Can't waltz to this one,' she said, and looked over his shoulder into the distance. Why was it that just when you seemed to come close to her, she disappeared? She had sat for ages listening to him, understanding everything. But it was as though she were afraid of being understood. The bark was prickly under his hand, and he knew he couldn't bear his weight on it much longer. He leant in closer to her face. She didn't move. The music wept (her eyes floated into his) and soared (she breathed in) and hovered (her lips were so close) and yearned (the smell of her skin and the bark filled his head) and lulled (he stared at her nose) and soared (he kissed her) and soared, and soared . . .

'I love you!'

'Don't be daft!'

He winced.

'I *do!*'

'That's ridiculous. You don't know me.'

He winced again. What a prat she must think him. He stood for a moment, cheeks burning, looking at her. Then he picked up his bicycle and turned.

'I'll prove it. You wait and see.'

He marched his bike across the field, past her car, past the herd of bullocks who were munching with provocative placidity. No sign of a trundle.

'Fuck off!' he said to one of them.

He started cycling energetically. There was still the ball, he thought. He had a plan there, possibly, if she went. He was near the main road, cycling hard and sweating copiously, when he let out a wail.

'Oh *no!*' he cringed. 'Oh God! No, no, *no!*' He had left the foul T-shirt by her side.

She could see he had been angry. He had spat the last words out, and fled. She noticed she was shaking. She sat down amongst the roots of the tree and looked at her painting things. Then she saw the vest and looked after Kieron, but he had gone. She picked it up and pressed her face into it. A wild, woody, unbearably addictive incense flooded her head.

Hearing

The entire school had been packed into a small medieval hall for the concert. The second part of *Elvira Madigan* began. The tremendous sudden presence of the music stunned her. She watched his fingers on the violin, her nostrils flared to breathe in the notes, her chest rose as she breathed. He caught her eye briefly. He did not smile, but she felt his pleasure of recognition. He inhaled proudly and floated into the music. She breathed deeply, trembling as the music flooded in. Kieron's whole body swayed, the piano *yearned*. The notes tripped over his fond fingers, eyelashes, nose, gently parted lips and the hair above his lip. And how the piano sighed, now softly, now heavily, and how she breathed, how she longed. Sitting there clutching her cardigan on her lap, waves of longing sweeping over her thickly, seeping into her, she did not notice that her eyes had filled with tears.

Love lost under the surface of the sea. Kieron was born on the third of June, nine months after Teddy Bowan went down to sleep on the bed of the ocean. Had some particles of him reached the shore where Kieron went in to save Elvis, scattering in the sunlit surf, settling as diamonds on the glistening body? Had he swallowed some in the salty rescue? Was he born of a dead lover's soul? She saw flesh nibbled by fish, and fish with strong dancing tails darting upstream to a waiting cavern. She closed her eyes and dreamt she found a pearl in an oyster. The pearl rolled gleaming in the palm of her hand and turned into a lover who smelt of sea and almonds. She heard the waves in the air.

Choosing

The phone rang in Eve's flat. It was Adrian, being passionate.
'Eve, I want to fuck you – really badly.'
'I only want to be fucked really well.'
'OK. Can I fuck you really well, then?'
'There's always a first time.'
He hung up.

Bottle

At Friday lunch-time Elvis was sitting on his bed knitting. Coriolanus Smith looked up from the opera he was composing.

'What are you doing?'

'I'm knitting.'

'Yes, but what?'

'A scarf.'

'Who for?'

'Matron.'

Coriolanus looked at the short rectangle of orange.

'It's not very long.'

'No, I'm getting quicker, though. I'm waiting for Matron to come and show me how to cast off, then I'll surprise her!'

Coriolanus thought Matron would certainly be surprised if she had to wear an orange coffee mat around her neck.

'I'm making one for Marilyn too,' said Elvis. 'I'll make you one if you like.'

The dormitory door was flung open, and Kieron said:

'I found Marilyn on the floor in the toilets!'

'Oh no!' Elvis put down his knitting, 'Is she ... OK?'

'I think so.'

Kieron pulled out a very small honey-coloured hamster from his pocket.

'She's not going to be secret much longer, Elvis – keep her in her cage under the bed, for Chrissakes.'

Elvis's guinea-pig, Boomer, had been thrown out by Cuthburtson because pets were not allowed in the boarding house. It had affected Elvis badly. This time he'd bought a hamster: something he could care for the way he would like to be cared for, the way Kieron did sometimes. He'd wanted something warm and cuddly too, and the picture Barnaby Wilson had on his study wall of Marilyn Monroe was just like that.

* * *

It was Friday afternoon again. Willy had gone off playing with guns, and Kieron was sitting in a corner of Folly's Yard talking to Joe. Folly's Yard was closing down because of lack of funding, and Kieron could hardly believe that Joe would have nowhere to go. Joe's best friend, Dunc, was almost in tears. He had just heard the bad news and was shouting obscenities at the authorities, or anyone who looked posh enough to be the authorities, like Kieron, for example.

'Don't mind him,' said Joe. 'Hey Dunc! He's all right – leave him!'

Kieron felt uncomfortable nonetheless. He couldn't help feeling there was something very wrong somewhere, and that, although it wasn't his fault, he should be doing something about it.

'But where will you go?' he asked Joe.

Joe looked at his lap, nodded, and said 'Aaah!' as if this explained everything. There was a long, friendly silence.

'A good place, really,' said Joe. 'Mind, you can't drink nothink in it.' He pulled a bottle out of his pocket and smiled. 'Empty, see.'

Kieron looked at the short flat bottle. On one side the back of a sailor had been painted, and on the other, the front of a naked woman with one of the sailor's hands on one huge breast and the other tucked into her crotch. Kieron had never seen anything quite like it, and stared at it, though not for as long as he would have liked to, in case it looked rude.

'What's that?'

'My bottle – goes everywhere with me.'

'Where did you get it? It's unusual.'

'Ah ... dunno. That I dunno. But I ent never gonna lose her, see. If I ever loses my bottle, I'll lose my bottle, see – get it? Ha, ha!'

He laughed with a chesty curdle, and Kieron laughed too. He admired Joe's bottle.

Before he left, Kieron gave Dunc a half-full packet of cigarettes and an unopened packet of chewing gum. Joe looked at Kieron curiously – perhaps sadly – so that Kieron took off his new Pearce House sports shirt and gave it to him. Joe nodded and smiled.

'I've only worn it once,' said Kieron, reassuringly.

But Joe didn't mind how many times he'd worn it.

Bubbles

She and Teddy had ridden white horses and circled the moon. They had had strawberry jelly on Venus and slept on Mars. They had read aloud to each other and chewed on grass. They had rolled down slopes and they had made love. They had made it, love, and it was still there, floating somewhere in space. Perhaps it was in the cracks of tree barks, in swallows' nests, in pen-nibs, in lovers' pockets, in pillow-cases or inside ears. Perhaps it showed itself in the glint of an eye or the curve of a smile. But they had made it, and it was there, waiting to be found again.

Kieron had given her many things, and those in object form she kept in a cupboard: a packet of chocolate buttons, a small model elephant, pressed rose petals, a cream egg, a book of stickers. They were all useless, yet he'd given them to her instinctively, like a cat who presents a dead bird or mouse at your feet, looking up in bewildered anticipation.

She opened the door to her cupboard of dead birds and looked at them. And as she did she felt she was opening a different door: one which opened from the inside. Trance-like, she made the wide step from the train to the platform.

'Come on, Eve, why do you keep making life so complicated for yourself? Maybe you don't really want a relationship.'

'Oh, cut out the analysis!'

Debbie was drying the dishes in Eve's flat and Eve was standing at the sink, washing laconically.

'Well, you could have anyone you wanted!'

'I hadn't noticed.'

'That's because you go off with men with mother problems, psychopaths, undersexed academics and pimply youths. There are loads of *normal* men out there capable of love and commitment.'

'The only men I've met capable of commitment aren't capable of spelling it.'

'Now you're being a pompous fart.'

'Sorry.'

'I suppose he's really bright, is he, this kid?'

'Yes, he is. Well ... he's imaginative.'

'He'd have to be to think you two could last.'

'Am I really being that stupid, Debs?'

'I'm afraid you are,' she flung down her tea-towel. 'No, not stupid. I can understand passion, believe me. But this is *madness*. It's such a *risk*, Eve.'

'How do you mean?'

'You'd lose your job...'

'Well...'

'...you'd lose your income, your mortgage, your flat, your car, your reputation ... Is that what you want?'

'No.'

'Well, that's what would happen. And what are you going to live off then, the pair of you? Love?'

'Well, what if we *did* manage to keep it a secret?'

'You wouldn't. Do you think a fifteen-year-old is going to keep quiet about a score like that? Do you really?'

'Sixteen-year-old.'

'Well, let's suppose he did. Let's suppose you're never found out. Let's suppose you don't *do* anything until he leaves school. Do you really want to be the granny at student parties? Do you want to spend each morning looking for new wrinkles? Do you want to live in fear of the day you're traded in – inevitably – for a younger model?'

'Inevitably?'

'Inevitably.'

'Lots of *older* men do that.'

'Well, find one that doesn't!'

'You're right. I'm looking for problems.'

'And what about him? You haven't thought about him! What if you find Mr Right in the middle of his "A" levels? Do you think he's going to forgive you for messing up his life?'

'There is no Mr Right.'

'He won't get over something like that in a hurry.'

'You're right.'

Immediately after telling Debbie she felt guilty. Not for anything between her and Kieron. She had the feeling that, in revealing things, she had somehow trivialised it all. She felt she had betrayed something; she had been disloyal to something fragile and beautiful.

'Oh, Eve, I'm sorry. But you must think about all these things. I don't want you getting hurt again.'

'Thanks.'

She picked up some bubbles from the suds in the sink, and watched them burst on her hand.

Fall Out

The Downleaze College Ball took place every year the week before Founder's Day and was a major social event in the region. Eve had decided not to go after her skirmish with Adrian and the recent humiliation at the school. But Adrian, who had previously thought the price of the tickets immoral and had sulked for days, now insisted that to waste them would be even more repugnant to him.

They were sitting at a table where 'younger' staff had been placed, presumably because they might have something in common. There was Avery and a Biology teacher called Stephan who talked about karate all evening, gave the girls marks out of ten for their bottoms, and got very drunk. There was a young maths teacher, fresh from his PGCE course, called Simon, who sat with his girlfriend Alison all evening. Simon and Alison seemed programmed to answer questions but not to ask any, so that any conversation felt like an interview. Then there was Adrian, who spent the evening railing against the garish displays of wealth and wasteful meat-eating, whilst becoming progressively drunk on champagne. And Eve, who sat uncomfortably garish and carnivorous in her bottle-green ball-gown.

The sixth-form girls were beautiful. They threw their shoulders back and their breasts out and sparkled. Radiance came easily to them, thought Eve. All they had to do was to open their mouths and smile. But she did not know that Cordelia, Amelia, Gemma, Emma and Edwina had been getting ready for the ball for three full days. Starting with new shoes, earrings and Wonderbra on Thursday, they had eyelash-dyed and exfoliated on Friday, leg-shaved, mud-packed and protein-serumed on Saturday, and by now they were like newly emerged butterflies whose former skins had been shed like last month's ball-gowns.

The appearance of Mr Oakey marked a turning point for Eve. She had not expected to see him, and to see him with a very handsome woman. But it was not Mr Oakey who disturbed Eve.

Fifth-form parents were only invited if they accompanied pupils. This couple's entry token would have been Kieron.

Adrian, who had refused to dance with Eve, was now asking unwilling sixth-form girls for fast numbers and trying to jitterbug to them. Spotting an opportunity, Felix sidled over and asked her to dance. She was tired of interviewing Simon and Alison, and wanted to see if the dance floor would give her a better view of who was there. But as she was considering grimly the prospect of any contact with Felix, she caught a figure moving towards Mr Oakey in her peripheral vision.

'I'm sorry, Felix,' she said. 'I'm not feeling well.'

'OK,' said Felix brightly, and asked Simon's girlfriend, who was not programmed to say 'no'.

Turning her head, she saw Kieron. He was looking at her. He rolled his eyes, smiled, and looked at his wine glass.

Adrian came and sat down heavily next to her, making unusually lewd comments about schoolgirls.

'Come and dance, you old bore!' he said, staggering to his feet and pulling her hand. She got up to avoid a scene, and danced self-consciously in the spot chosen by Adrian, directly in front of the Oakeys' table. Adrian kept losing his balance and she was afraid to desert him. Mr Oakey smiled at her, and she smiled back, ashamed. Kieron gave her a stabbing stare, and when she had rotated one more time he had gone from the table. Now she had to finish the wretched dance, wondering where he was.

Her angry panic took Eve by surprise. The next song was one of her favourites and she knew he would be dancing it with Cordelia or some other newly dehisced flower. She left Adrian sandwiched between two women and went to circle the marquee. All she could see were the backs of people dancing around the edge of the dance floor. He could have been any one of the heads bobbing in the middle. She caught sight of Willy, stuck to a tall girl in pink like a fly on a lolly. He must be nearby. It was only a matter of time and Kieron would be stuck to someone too. Then she saw him, jumping around with a girl in blue. All she could see through the mist of dancers and music was the girl in blue with her perfect back and her sleek brown hair. She waited, motionless, for glimpses of her nose, her teeth, her eyes, as she bounced around Kieron, shamefully hoping for some gross facial disfigurement. But the girl was perfect. What could this blue girl see in Kieron? He was only sixteen and there were plenty of sixth formers there for the likes of her. What was she doing with him? She didn't know the honey of his armpits and the secrets of his dreams. *Did* she? Or had he come with her? Of course he had. All that love crap ... She was so stupid! How could she imagine, how could she dare to imagine that an old hag like herself...? She went to sit down.

She looked at her sequinned bag on the table. It was trash. She'd had it for years and it was out of date. Her shoes were old and the sparkle was peeling off. She had made her dress seven years ago and had worn it to every ball since – all two of them. She wanted to talk to Kieron but she wasn't worthy of him. She was shabby, she was poor, and most of all, she was *OLD*.

Men in clumps around the marquee burst into guffaws about a shared joke, a cricket yarn, her shabby dress, her age ... Women bobbed out of corners on springs, red lips gleaming, like Jack-in-the-boxes, cackling at her shame. People laughed everywhere, their pig squeals shrill around the buffet, their teeth shining like hyenas'. The compère announced it was time for some classical music. The entire dance floor cleared, and the strains of Strauss seemed to mock her with premeditated cruelty. She went in search of some air.

'Who's that utter dickhead you're with?'

A hand touched the inside of her elbow as she reached an open flap in the marquee. Every nerve in her body ended at that small patch of elbow. It was Kieron.

'Oh, that's Adrian.'

'Who's he? Your boyfriend?'

'No. Not at all.'

Kieron smiled.

'Are you with your girlfriend?'

'I am now,' he said, giving her elbow a squeeze.

'No, I mean, who was that girl?'

'Dunno. Some friend of Willy's.'

'She's very beautiful.'

'Thick as pigshit, though!'

She smiled. They were quiet for a moment, taking the air. Kieron picked at the guy-rope.

'I feel like a clown,' he said.

'Why?'

'This dinner jacket is about ten times too big for me – I look ridiculous.'

'You look lovely.'

'What did you say?'

'I said you don't look ridiculous.'

Kieron smiled all over.

'This is our tune,' he said. 'Remember?' and he led her on to the empty dance floor to waltz to Strauss.

They moved easily together without the thistles or cow-pats. That they should have dared to dance at all attracted attention, but that they were alone on the dance floor for over a minute before a few parental couples joined them attracted even more attention. For this reason they didn't speak again. The waltz galloped and bounded, tripped and teased. They moved on wings through the pedestrian couples, smiling, trying not to smile. The hyenas were no more. They glided in graceful unison.

Then something happened.

Mr Oakey, stroking the rim of his wine glass, noticed it first; Felix, eating his third plate of cold meat, put down his fork in panic; Mrs Craven's mouth hung motionless in slow, horror-filled recognition; Mr Craven saw it too, about the time he finished lighting his cigar; the headmaster's wife, who hadn't stopped socialising all evening, fell silent; Mrs Cuthburtson welled up with such emotion that she felt she would choke. They had all seen it and there was no mistaking it. It threatened everything; it confused the proper order of things; its fall-out shook the poles of the marquee: the look Kieron Oakey and Eve Swanbrook had exchanged was a look of love.

Casting Off

Matron was leaning against some cupboards in her kitchen, showing Elvis how to cast off. Kieron was throwing pieces of biscuit in the air for her dog. She was about forty-five and beautiful, and very wise (she always knew when you were lying). There wasn't *much* you couldn't tell Matron over a cup of Ovaltine.

'Do you think when someone marries someone a lot older it means they're looking for a parent figure?' asked Kieron.

She administered some aspirin to a boy with earache, and he thought she had forgotten to answer him. But she sent the boy away and replied:

'Not necessarily.'

'Why do they do it, then?'

'Because they love each other,' she said simply. 'Anyway, why are you so interested?'

'I'm not really. I was just thinking of the headmaster and his wife. I mean, he's a lot older than her, isn't he? *They're* not in love, are they?'

'Oh, she married him for status. That's different. And he probably wouldn't have got promotion if he hadn't been married.'

'So age doesn't matter then, you reckon?'

'Oh, *age* doesn't matter a jot. The thing is, it's the *pattern* of a relationship that matters. A woman can be the same age as a man but still marry him because he reminds her of her father, or treats her like a daughter. And the same with a man. Seeing someone as a father-figure or a mother-figure has got nothing to do with age.'

Kieron stopped throwing food for the dog and looked thoughtful. The dog started yelping, and he teased it with some more biscuit.

'Why is it OK for a man to be older than a woman and not the other way round, then?'

'Well, that's men for you, isn't it! There's nothing wrong with it either way round, if you ask me. I expect it used to have something to do with financial security. One of those taboos we have to cast off, I suppose. Don't tell anyone this – no, perhaps I'd better not say...'

'Go on – we won't tell anyone – promise.'

'Well, (and don't let this go outside this room, mind), I answered an ad in a personal column once, and this man (he'd sent me a really dishy photo of himself – wow!) he said on the phone (he was *forty-four*, mind): "I think it only fair to tell you that I'm looking for a partner between twenty-five and thirty-five years of age. There are practical and personal reasons for this, so I hope you won't be offended if you don't meet this requirement"!' She burst out laughing and added: 'And *he* was forty-four. He *required* that his partner should be *at least* fourteen years younger than him, and preferably twenty! What a bugger!'

'What did you do?'

She stood very tall. 'I told him where to go! And do you know what?'

'What?'

'I *was* only twenty-five at the time!'

Elvis, who was sitting on the table, suddenly asked:

'Would you consider marrying someone a *lot* younger than yourself, Matron?'

'Oh, I require it,' she laughed. 'You mean someone about, say ... thirteen?' she winked at Kieron.

Elvis shrugged bashfully, without taking his eyes from his casting off.

'Possibly,' he said.

Eve was sipping tea with Arthur Hope.

'Call me Arthur.'

'Arthur ... could I ask you for some advice?'

'Of course.'

Arthur settled into his chair. There was nothing he loved more than tea and advice with women, and especially this one.

'If you were in love with someone entirely inappropriate and ... well ... if they were in love with you too ... and no one else was getting hurt, then would it be wrong?'

He smiled in every crease of his face. 'Of course not – how could it be wrong?'

It had been a ridiculous question and she shouldn't have asked him.

'We're not talking adultery here, are we?'

'No.'

'Just checking,' he looked relieved. 'No one else getting hurt?'

'No one.'

'I don't understand how it could be wrong.'

'We're only talking hypothetically, you understand.'

'Of course.'

'But ... if there were an age-gap between you ...'

He peered at her across the clear space of fifty years, and danced into her eyes.

'Age makes no difference in love. Love is ... anarchical!'

'But it might.'

'How?'

'A big age-gap might.'

'My dear –' his gaze landed gently on the down of her neck – 'no. We always find some excuse to turn our back on love. We analyse too much. If it's not age it's class, or religion, or income. There was a woman once ... she loved me ... Don't think about it too much. Just let it in.'

He got up slowly and went over to his record-player in the corner.

'There's only one thing that makes people old.'

'What's that?'

'They stop growing. A rose grows until it shrivels. As long as you keep growing, you don't age, I say.'

A record fell quietly on to the turntable.

'You know what they say about old dogs.'

'You can't teach an old dog new tricks?'

'That's right. Well, if you keep learning new tricks, you can't be an old dog, either,' he chuckled. 'May I?'

He indicated a waltz with her, and they waltzed around the room singing 'Waltzing on Clouds'. He spun her round and round and into the hall and out on to the patio and on to the lawn and around the gnomes. Waltzing, waltzing, waltzing round gnomes. She smelt the vanilla of tobacco in his old jacket. She looked into his green, glinting eyes and at the tuft of strong white hair sticking up from his head, and she wondered if she wasn't in love with him too.

Ear, Nose and Throat

Kieron knew that Miss Swanbrook had asked for helpers in the Art display for Founder's Day. He knew that she wanted helpers between four p.m. and six p.m. on Friday, and he knew that Elvis and Tuckman, a pear-shaped boy with breasts from the fourth form who wasn't in any of the teams, would have volunteered. At 5.55 p.m. he waited at the bottom of the stairs leading up to the Art room. At 6.03 he heard Elvis and Tuckman coming down, and he watched from the safety of an archway as they scampered and waddled off to supper in the rain. Then he climbed the stone steps two at a time and poked his head around the Art room door, gasping for breath.

There was no one there. He leant his arm on the wall and rested his head on it, catching his breath in disappointment. Two tall facing walls were covered in life-drawings, fruit, animal skulls and bizarre abstracts with one-word titles in pastels, oils and ink. The other two walls were shortened by the sloping glass roof which made the Art room the brightest in the building. The easels had been stacked in one corner or set in groups to display work. In another corner, the huge mattress on which the life models (for sixth form only) lay sprawled for long sessions on washed-out crimson velvet curtains with a small electric fire to roast them. Kieron eyed it with a gush of forlorn lust.

Suddenly a door at the opposite end of the room opened and Ecstasy appeared from the narrow room linking her Art room to the second Art room and the Ceramics centre.

'I'm afraid you're too late, I was just going.'

Kieron had thought it all through carefully and was ready for this one.

'Actually, I had something to ask you.'

'What's that?' Miss Swanbrook was rattling her keys and turning towards the door from which she had just emerged.

'Do you think I could do "A" level Art next year?'

'Of course you could. You know you're capable, surely. The thing is to consider what you want to do eventually...'

'No – I know I want to do it. What I was wondering, was whether you could tell me about the course and that. It's not just drawing and painting, is it?'

Eve felt uncomfortable about spending any time alone with Kieron after the brush with the headmaster, and she knew this was manufactured time alone. She looked thoughtful, and opened the door again.

'I can lend you a book if you like – about some artists we cover.'

She was running her finger along a bookshelf at eye level, and Kieron slipped in through the door behind her.

He had never been in this booky-smelling room before. Along both sides of the wall were long desks covered in coffee mugs, skulls, shells and papers; above these were cork boards with posters of Art exhibitions pinned haphazardly to them; above these were bookshelves stretching up to the ceiling, holding heavy books with fat, colourful bindings, boxes of labelled past papers and bulging ringbinders. Kieron looked at a human skull which smiled eyelessly back at him. Eve selected a book, flicked through it, and presented it wordlessly to Kieron.

'Is that it?'

'Yes,' she said coldly, still not facing him. 'You'll get a taste of what we study from that. You'd better go now.'

'What's the matter?'

'What do you mean?'

'You're in a pretty shitty mood.'

Eve turned to him.

'There are some words in your vocabulary, Kieron Oakey, that you would do well to eliminate. One of them is "shitty".'

'Which one's that, Miss?' He smiled impishly, sat down on the desk, and looked at the book.

'Ho! Ho!' she said dryly, looking at his bent head pretending to read the book. She couldn't help but be struck by his nose, his ears, his neck.

Oh, wondrous nose! Oh gentle, flawless, nasal simplicity! The so-slightly curved line of the profile, the marble curves of the nostrils, the utter, unforgivable nonchalance of its modest owner.

Oh ears! Twirled silk delving deep into the very soul of him. Trumpeting from each side of his head, beckoning, teasing, disappearing into the unknown tunnels of his dreams.

Oh!

Promising

He sat so close that she could smell the warm oily odour of his wet hair and the damp wool of his clothes.

It was about that time that the old porter, having checked to see there was no one in the Art room, locked the door from the outside and went to the video room to watch Emmerdale.

Time

Arthur Hope was in love. It was the feeling he'd had once a long time ago. It was the feeling he'd had for Deanna all these years, but this time it was for someone tangible again, real. If only he were fifty years younger. Fifty years! Did they really matter? What had he achieved in them? And if he found, on reflection, that he had achieved nothing much in those years, wouldn't it be fair for them just to drop away?

Fifty years since he was thirty-five. And in that time he'd had two daughters and a wife that died on him. Neither daughter visited him. He threw down his magazine and got up from his chair. His hand rested on the velvet cushion he'd been sitting on, stroking it softly. He felt the impression where his behind had been, and wondered if it were greater than the impression he'd left on either of his daughters, or on anyone. One daughter, Ariadne, had married a marine biologist and lived in New Zealand with liver trouble. And Ruth, his pride and joy (little Ruth with the rosy cheeks who liked to play giddy-up on his knees), had become a lesbian social psychologist, author of *Our Parents' Debt*, a book about the colossal guilt religious parents bore for screwing up the lives of their offspring.

Not a lot to account for fifty years. And fifty years was all that kept him from the object of all his affections: Eve Swanbrook. Yes, he was sure it was just time. Time, that unseeable, intangible, inaudible, tasteless, odourless nothingness; yet mighty divider of people, colossal slaughterer of hope and opportunity.

His eyes caught the heading of a magazine article: 'Going for Old: Antiques aren't just for collectors...'

He ripped out the offending page and tore it into tiny bits, which he scattered over the living room, hall and kitchen. Then he took out his old Hoover and vacuumed them up, wanting to vacuum up time.

A Funny Thing

Kieron was fingering the lock.

'Don't you have a key?'

She did, but it only opened the door from the outside. He muttered as he examined the blank, flat piece of steel, unable to believe that there was a key-hole on the outside only: a safety lock. He seemed determined to get it open and Eve, unreasonably shocked by all this talk of locks and keys and prising things open, retreated to the inner sanctum of the book room.

On learning that the door had been locked from the outside, Eve had felt a sudden, sickening dismay. She was unprepared for this forced intimacy and uneasy at its implications. The gossip, the guilt, the pointed finger, the punishing headlines. She felt the glorious erotic suspense of whatever there was between them being crushed under the sharp hoof of reality. She could see it all clearly as she looked around the Art room. There would be weak attempts to get out, the mutual shyness, the blushes, the coy glances, the inevitable night on the models' mattress (so near yet so far), the hugging for warmth, and then *it*. And what about it? How would it be? All this longing, loving, lusting, dreaming – what *was* it? – all over, wasted, spoiled, squandered in a few fumbling, unshocking seconds. She saw it, hopelessly, as she sighed heavily and flared her nostrils, trying to locate the precise cause of her distress. She moved uneasily about the room, looking for ways out.

After five minutes, he was still to be heard attacking the lock. He was persistent, then, you had to give him that.

Kieron was trying to hack a hole in the surround frame large enough to look as though he were trying to open the door. He was playing for time, mumbling to himself about mortice deadlocks, boxed locking-plates and door-jambs. He knew he wouldn't get the door open. For one thing it was impossible: it was indeed a safety lock. For another, he had absolutely no intention of opening it. An occasion like this didn't present itself very often, and for a moment he even fondly imagined that Ecstasy had set it up herself, until he remembered how he had planned the encounter and how fidgety and pissed off she seemed right now. It left him in a deep quandary. It was great getting this far – a miracle – with your fantasy woman, but only assuming she hadn't turned into some kind of Miss Safeway figure, turning on the schoolmistress clap-trap and shooting you knuckle-rapping glances that froze you to the door-frame. So that was it. She was delineating her territory and keeping him well back in his classroom place: you boy, me woman. He considered that it might be even more terrifying if she *did* behave as his fantasy woman, but he had to take this tiny slither of a chance, because the possible rewards were so high. The *potential*, as he would have said to Willy, was endless. But all that was before he had these feelings for her, and now nothing would ever be quite the same again. Even so ... The situation might be fraught with difficulties, but it had presented itself, and it was promising. He left the aching wound of the door and went to find Ecstasy.

Arthur Hope was standing in the living room ironing his surplice. It had already been washed and pressed by Mrs Platt, but he had spilt tea over it trying it on in practice. The gathering near the neck was the tricky bit.

'Ladies and Gentlemen, boys – and girls – Governors, Head-master...' he said to himself, poking the tip of the iron into the folds. No. Headmaster and governors first, perhaps?

'You know, a funny thing happened to me the other day...'

He put down the iron and clasped the edge of the ironing board as if it were the pulpit, and wagged a storyteller's finger at the blank television. Then he looked at the Swiss clock above the television: it ticked and tocked like the Rolexes of the waiting crowd. (A bit of dramatic tension was important.)

'You know, a funny thing happened to me the other day...'

He looked across at the mantelpiece, at the little wooden letter-holder containing news dating back to before his wife died. He stared at the small copper ornament depicting a coal-basket they'd brought back from their honeymoon in Swansea. It needed a clean. He stared at the fireplace and gripped the edge of the ironing board hard with trembling knuckles. Ladies and Gentlemen, nothing had happened to him the other day. Nothing had happened to him for a very long time. And it was a funny thing.

This Is Serious

They sat sipping coffee from two chipped mugs.

'Someone will come in the morning, don't worry,' he said, sitting cross-legged on the mattress. 'You don't like it here, do you?'

She looked across at him from her desk.

'Here doesn't like me.'

'Why do you say that? We all like you.' He wanted to add 'especially me', but she wasn't in the mood. 'Elvis is mad about you. He's always talking about you.'

'Is he all right, do you think? Is there something upsetting him?'

'Cuthburtson, I think. God, Cuthburtson's a bastard. He's always punishing Elvis.'

'Why?'

'Dunno. Likes it, I suppose. Easy target. You know one of his favourite punishments? He's got this rucksack with bricks *sewn* into it, and you have to run across the bridge and back as often as he wants you to.'

'What's to stop you taking it off?'

'Ah, that's where he's a really cunning bastard. He gets to know all the toll-bridge men, and he rings them up to say you're coming. Then they'll only give you a ticket if you're running up wearing the thing. And you don't finish your punishment until you've got, say, three tickets, or however many circuits he wants you to do.'

'That's awful!'

'Yip!' Kieron felt very comfortable now.

'Tell me something. Why did Mr Culpin leave?'

'He was gay,' said Kieron, stretching out in a worldly manner. 'But he didn't do anything to us. I mean we didn't know he was gay, really. It was Cuthburtson who let that little gem out of the bag, just to punish him. They had some disagreement – Mr Culpin knew too much, I think, about Cuthburtson. He tried to complain about his punishments, and Cuthburtson got him sent away. But he never touched *anyone* – not that I know of, anyway. Not like Cuthburtson.'

'How do you mean?'

'He's a pervert.'

He took off his tracksuit top and made himself more comfortable. Eve looked at Kieron, lying out on the mattress before her, and felt uneasy again. She had a suspicion that her feelings had become masters of themselves: they could wave defiantly, they could make her jump through hoops, they could give her rides to heaven.

She went into the small closet used by artists' models, removed a tube from her shopping bag and washed her teeth with hair-removing cream. She came out angrily, bearing hairless, plaque-free teeth.

'Look, Kieron. I don't know what you're playing at but this is serious.' Her tongue throbbed and her lips were glowing. Masters of themselves. 'My job's on the line. First you get into my flat, then we get into the newspaper, and now we're locked up alone all night in my room. It's gone past the joke, Kieron. Are you listening to me? I've had it with you!'

'I can't remember that,' he shrugged playfully. 'Can we have it again?'

The Reverend Mr Hope was clamping a tea-towel to his head with a tie and saying: 'Ladies and Gentlemen ... Who do I remind you of? Young man in the front row ... yes ... you ... No, not a sheik – try again ... Yes, the woman with the ridiculous hat ... yes, you madam, that's right ... JESUS. Jolly good.' He picked up the iron and breathed out, 'Jesus!'

He went over to an occasional table and removed an umbrella plant from its pot. Crumbs of earth spilt on the floor as he placed the rooty clump on the table, and the pot on his head.

'I used to do miracles, you know – just like that! Jusslikethat!' He tittered and sat down heavily on the sofa behind him, and sighed, 'Jesus Christ!'

Feet

———◆———

'It's hot,' she said, lifting her dress away from her skin.

Now what was she doing? She was sitting on the draining board with her feet in the massive white enamel sink. He wanted to join her on the opposite draining board, but this would mean taking his shoes off and his socks smelt.

He disappeared into the closet and saw a loo and a tiny washbasin the shape of a kidney bean. He stood with one foot high in the basin and the other one on the mat, soaping the grooves between his toes impatiently. Trying to swap them around he slipped with some balletic splits and brought the kidney bean clattering to the ground. He nursed his balls wordlessly and prayed he hadn't damaged anything crucial. Next door water was crashing into the huge sink.

'You OK?' she said as he returned limping.

'Fine.'

'Thought you might have hurt yourself for a moment.'

'Nope.'

He climbed up on to the opposite draining board and dipped a toe gingerly into the cold water. Her small feet were wading about and some water was seeping up the cloth at her hemline. The evening sun turned her ankles to gold. He placed both feet in boldly. He turned the taps off (amazing himself how he could take control). The silence seemed to be announcing the start of something, and he was certain they both felt it. The hush before the curtains open.

He shuffled his feet.

'It's so hot!' she said again, pushing out her bottom lip and blowing the hair off her face.

'Yeah,' he said, doing the same.

He shuffled his feet some more, and she wiggled her toes. They both looked down, to avoid looking at each other.

Eve was not sure about all this foot and toe intimacy. If he was

159

going to make a move, why didn't he just get on with it? Then she could give a decisive rebuff. Or not. No, definitely. Unthink it. One of her toenails was going yellow and she had hairs sprouting above her ankles which she hadn't noticed out of water. She could feel a trickle of sweat run down behind her knees and her lips were raw from the depilatory cream. She was sure her faint moustache showed in the sunlight and a sting on her cheek made her remember a slight spot which was probably pustular by now. Probably more than anyone he thought that women were dolls, angels. She didn't want to see the look of disappointment (horror?) when he realised she was only a sweaty hirsute woman with swollen lips and an erupting spot. So she looked down at her feet. But it wouldn't go away.

She was a doll! She had glorious goose-pimples and tiny feet and he didn't know what to do. It would have been OK if they'd just gone to bed or something. He would have known at least what he was *supposed* to do. But no one ever told you what you were supposed to do with a woman sitting opposite you with her feet in cold water wiggling her toes, or that when big feet were put next to little feet they seemed so much bigger and so much smaller and that just looking at them can make you feel powerful. They seemed to just get bigger and bigger. And it wouldn't go away. Everything seemed to be growing and growing and giving him away. He slid into the vast sink. His tracksuit and shirt became heavy beneath the water. He splashed her until she too was sodden. Then she got up and fell back on the jam-jars behind her with a clatter. (When you were stuck you could always fall back on jam-jars.) She laughed but she didn't move. Was it ever going to happen?

She suggested drying their wet, swollen clothes in the kiln, on a low heat. They dressed separately in velvet curtain togas and folded their clothes neatly for a slow roast.

There was a silence. The hush before the curtains opened.

He tried to entice her over to the mattress by lying on it and pointing up to the ceiling.

'What's that?'

A huge dark painting on cloth covered one part of the sloped roof.

'It's "The Moon and the Stars",' she said. 'Third form did it.'

But she remained with her back to him at the bookcase. He went and picked up a skull on the table beside her, running his fingers around the eye sockets and making the jaw move.

'Life's too short...' he said at last, and the unspoken words to finish the sentence hung in the air and repeated themselves like an echo. She looked at Colin, and wondered who he had been once, if he had been happy, or if birds had pecked away at his flesh before anything had begun for him. Then she moved her eyes to an Art book open in her hand. Kieron pored over it too, catching intense glimpses of the text and ignoring them.

'I like this one,' he pointed arbitrarily to a woman reading.

HIS PAINTINGS ARE INNOCENT, ANODYNE, BUT STRANGELY ENGAGÉS

'Yes, I like that one too. Look at the use of colour. Look at her pose ... She has a wonderful quality ...'

SHE IS LUSTY, SELF-ABSORBED, YET CURIOUSLY INGÉNUE

'I'd like to be able to paint like that.'

'And why not?'

'Oh, I couldn't. Do you think I could? Ever?'

'You would have your own style but ... why don't you try? If you really want to...'

'I do. I have this urge and it won't go away.'

'Then you should.'

'I will.'

'No, I mean you really should. If it won't go away.'

'It won't.'

'Do it then.'

'OK. Do you think...?'

'I do.'

'Really?'

'Yes.'

HIS PAINTING RELENTLESSLY PROPELS US TO THE INEVITABLE RAPTURE OF ITS SUBTEXT.

Heavenly Bodies

At 3.02 a.m. Iona Craven was reading the penultimate chapter of a novel. Her sister had phoned from Australia at 2.50 a.m. to say that her nephew had won a scholarship to Cambridge, and now she couldn't get to sleep. In the penultimate chapter a handsome (but cruel) impoverished young doctor was revealing his true nature to a wise and cautious young journalist who had been posted to the same wretched remote island as the handsome young doctor. And in fact, he wasn't cruel after all. Or impoverished (his aunt having left him an island in the second paragraph), but he did maintain his cruel piercing look in order to melt the young journalist who was not so cautious after all.

At 3.02 Jeremy Lancelot was also throwing caution to the wind. Unable to sleep because his wife had the bedside lamp on, he had gone tentatively to the bathroom. At 3.02 he stood against the door with some Andrex, accidentally knocking some hair conditioner into the bath with a clatter.

At 3.02 a.m. the moon slipped out from behind a cloud and Marilyn the hamster, who had been gnawing at her cage bars all night in quite a frisky fashion, and who was still only very small, made her way through the bent bars, whiskers a-tremble, and plopped idly on to the bare boards of Pearce House third-form dormitory.

At 3.02 a.m. Felix's eyelids flickered in the darkness of his dream-filled bed. He was standing on the quay and a large boat with everyone on it was stealing slowly away. He was trying to get on but the gap between the boat and the quay was widening. The boat glided off, and he was left with his suitcase, waving after it on the quayside.

At 3.02 the dark figure of a beggarman rolled over on a bench in the shopping precinct, and his lolling arm knocked over the half-full bottle on the pavement, sending an early morning bird – or a late night one – fluttering through the cool air.

Promising

At 3.02 the dawn chorus filled the Art room. Kieron leant over and kissed her goodnight.

It was quick. It was sweet. It was endless. Each second was made of elastic and stretched and stretched until it was all let go. TWANG. BOING. They both lay momentarily unconscious. A large watermelon and a wooden bowl had fallen on them from a still life. Then the Stars and the Moon fell down from the ceiling on to their hot wet happy limbs.

Shouting from the Rooftops

They slept little, whispering through the dawning hours.

He had watched her sleeping, trying not to miss a moment, but had fallen asleep in the scent of her neck. He awoke to the smell of it. He felt whole. He felt a man. Everything was perfect. He didn't want variety. He wanted this. He wanted more of the same, over and over. He could be locked in a room with her for ever: there would be no loneliness there. He could travel for miles in her eyes. With her he could remain as still as a tree and travel anywhere. He said one word and she understood the twenty left unsaid. And just lying there, the earth had turned around almost one half. How many miles per hour had they been spinning at? By tonight it would have turned around completely, as his world had changed. He loved her.

She was surprised when she woke, curled in the curve of his lap, that she had slept at all. She saw the long fingers entwined in hers: they were Kieron's, and she was glad. She smiled at all the claims of lovers: the measure of a true lover was his capacity to love. All the love ever made in the world had gathered there; it had come out from secret places everywhere on earth and in the air and converged on Kieron, nestled in him as he curved around her. He had let her climb into his heart and see the delights he planned for her. He gave everything. He watched her carefully. His eyes could read the stars of her soul, and he knew the way. He smelt of wood and musk; he smelt of sea and almonds. Kieron had touched her, and she let herself be loved.

When the warm morning filled the Art room, Kieron went in search of his clothes, determined to find a way through the skylight before they were discovered. He found the garments in small cooked pieces in the kiln, where they had left them.

'Kieron?' called Eve. 'Where are you?'

'Just getting our clothes,' he said, approaching with a portion of burnt dress which fell apart as he held it up to her.

'Oh.'

'We'll have to make do with the curtains. I think I've found a way out. If we're quick, we'll make it before anyone finds us.'

He climbed on the table in the book room and hacked at the skylight with a piece of wood. She wrapped her toga around her and followed him.

'Not the skylight.'

'Why not?'

'We can't get down from the roof – it's miles up.'

He was on a chair on the table, and was poking his head out into the open.

'Aha! But there's scaffolding all round the chapel. All we have to do is get across to the chapel roof.'

'Aren't you clever!'

He started to hum James Bond theme music and pulled her through the skylight, kissing her naked shoulders and holding her tight. They slithered awkwardly down to the parapet and walked along the wide guttering towards the chapel roof. Easy. Then there was just the ten-foot gap between the two roofs, bridged only by scaffolding. Eve's insides rotated. They were very high up.

'Just think of it as a climbing frame,' said Kieron. 'Follow me – take your time.'

He crawled along the scaffold and waited for Eve. She went very still.

'What's the matter?'

'Listen!'

They listened. Inside the chapel a hymn had just begun. It was later than they thought. The Founder's Day service was under way.

'Quick!'

She looked down at the ground beneath her and closed her eyes. Slowly she grasped the cold iron of the scaffold and inched her way along, clinging on with everything.

'I feel ridiculous,' she said.

'You don't look ridiculous,' he said helpfully. 'You look lovely.'

And with that she fell, rolling around the scaffold so that she looked like a beast on a spit.

'Shit!'

'Christ! Hang on! Hang on! I'm coming – just stay still.' He made his way towards her.

'Actually, you do look a bit ridiculous now.'

'I'm dying!'

'You know, falling in dreams means you're falling in love.'

'Oh God! Please tell me this is a dream!'

He had reached her, and the sky swung around.

'I've got you – just stay still.'

And as he freed both of his arms to pull her up, his velvet toga dropped away and floated regally in the wind, landing, as they watched, on a golden cross.

The cross was moving! Arthur Hope was carrying it out of chapel, leading the choir and the rest of the congregation into the chapel quadrangle. Looking up at his red flag, Arthur broke off the chanting. ('Four-leaved Clover twenty to one!' Mr Cox could be heard saying to himself, unaware, with his earphone in, that the choir had stopped singing.) This was a sign from God, thought Arthur mischievously, and he started singing to himself ('...We'll keep the red flag flying here...') without really thinking. Some of the choir, confused, followed him in song, the rest smirked, and one or two looked up to see the culprits on the roof.

Soon the entire congregation had spilled out into the quadrangle, set for the social mingling of the year. But no sooner had they started mingling, holding on to their hats in the wind, than there was a flurry of disturbance amongst the crowd. Soon all eyes were turned up to the roof, to a naked sixteen-year-old and a woman hanging upside down in a red velvet curtain, exposing greater or lesser views of lingerie according to the wind. (Ian McCaskill had been right.)

'Eve, my *darling*!' shouted Arthur Hope, seeing her. 'What *are* you doing?'

'I was just...' she could barely hold on.

The congregation swam beneath her. Tanned faces in pretty hats; green, pink, blue, violet coats and dresses; dark suits and crisp white shirts; expressions all alarmed, all turned up to her.

'It's not what it seems.'

What *did* it seem like? Nobody had any idea. The crowd was droning loudly.

'You look *lovely*, my dear. You look just like Mary Poppins!' and Arthur Hope started to hum. Then he started to sing with all his lung capacity, filling the echoing quadrangle: 'Chim chiminey, chim chiminey, chim chim cheroo...' Leading the younger members of the choir who didn't dare disobey him. A staff member of the choir cuffed the smallest choirboy and told him to belt up.

A man with an expensive coat said to his wife: 'This is a

madhouse.' But he carried on looking up in case the wind blew up again. 'An absolute madhouse.'

'What on EARTH do you think you are doing?' yelled the headmaster, angry because his wife would be angry if he didn't show his authority.

Kieron beat his chest and swung from a handy rope emitting a breath-taking, Tarzan-like howl. He swept Eve up in his arms in one swoop and saved her from falling, kicking the headmaster to the ground as he completed the swing. The crowd gasped and looked on in admiration as he beat his chest again: 'I LOVE HER!'

'What?' whimpered the headmaster, writhing on the ground in agony. 'You'll be expelled for this!'

'I don't care! I LOVE HER – do you hear everyone? I LOVE HER!!!'

'We're stuck,' said Kieron instead.

The groundsmen were called to fetch a ladder.

Matron's Scarf

There were pre-lunch sherry parties arranged in each boarding house after chapel, and the headmaster did not want his own schedule disturbed by the fiasco. He had therefore sent for Kieron to see him at two o'clock, and asked Cuthburtson to deal with him in the meantime. He asked Mrs Cuthburtson to deal with Miss Swanbrook: he would deal with *her* later.

Mrs Cuthburtson was standing in front of her wardrobe going through her clothes.

'This might do for you,' she said gently, turning round and holding out a light blue dress. 'I'm afraid I've grown out of it. It's a bit fuddy-duddy, I suppose, but I don't think I have a lot else that would fit you.'

'Thank you. It's very kind of you. I'm so *sorry* about all this. It's really not as bad as it seems. We were locked in by mistake...'

'Don't you worry. You get some clothes on – you must be freezing!'

She turned to the window while Eve put the dress over her head.

'What do you think they'll do – about Kieron, I mean? Will he be expelled?' asked Eve.

'I don't know. I've just seen him go out now. David's sent him off with those wretched bricks strapped to his back.' Her voice grew strangely bitter. 'He's so barbaric sometimes.'

'You sound as if you don't approve.'

Mrs Cuthburtson dropped the piece of net curtain she was holding back and continued to talk to the window.

'I used to think my father was God.' She was distant and expressionless, fingering the petals of the flowers in the curtain print. 'I married a man like my father.' She turned to face Eve. 'And now,' she sighed, 'I don't believe in God any more.'

Eve stood, befrocked in blue, and looked across the vast double bed at Mrs Cuthburtson. The sherry party was in full swing and people were laughing and talking loudly beneath their feet. She wanted to put her arm around her. Instead she said:

'I won't embarrass you by coming down. Cuth ... David asked me to make myself scarce...'

'Nonsense. You're coming down with me. You haven't done anything wrong.'

There was a lavish display of food in the dining room, and Matron was chopping up fruit for the Pimms in the corner. She was feeling like a slave. She was always invited to these do's with a posh card as if she was some special guest, and she always ended up being used like a servant. Elvis and another boy were taking Pimms around on trays.

The talk was all of the scene on the roof. The latest story was that terrorists had held them at gun-point in the Art room. Most weren't swallowing this, and one or two parents were calling for her immediate dismissal.

Eve confined herself to a corner behind the stairs, afraid she might spark off a marital row if Cuthbertson saw her. But people seemed to avoid speaking to her, with the result that Elvis offered her endless drinks from his tray. Soon she was on another planet. One particularly belligerent man approached her at this point. She recognised him as the father of a boy in her third-form Art set.

'I'm afraid I shall want my son to change sets.'

She heard 'change sex' and looked confused.

'Well, I'd advise him to think about it very carefully first – it's irreversible.'

'I hope so.'

'And it'll cost a fortune.'

'Are you bribing me?'

'What? Quite frankly, it's of no interest to me whether he does or not,' she frowned at him. 'Well, actually I can't see him in a skirt at all.'

Mrs Cuthburtson kindly offered to take Eve upstairs where she could bring her some food, and Eve was about to accept with relief when there was a shocking scream. All talking stopped, and faces turned in the direction of the large dining room table.

Marilyn was sitting on the corner of the table, cheeks filled with peanuts, angular lumps poking through the fur. At the sound of the scream she stopped dead, whiskers trembling, paws clasping a peanut like a hunchbacked wise man proffering his incense. Cuthburtson picked up an empty wine bottle and raised it high over the hamster's head. Elvis ran forward. Down came the bottle, down, down, down ... Elvis-height, and there was a growling wail, 'Waaah!' as the long dark bottle, grabbed by Elvis, landed in Cuthburtson's crotch. Elvis stared at the bottle. The Blue Nun stared back at him from the label, wine gushed out from its neck. And then, in the thickening silence, he whacked the throbbing genitals again ... and again, and again, until a sixth-former with a tassel came and gripped his arms.

Cuthburtson was lying on the floor wincing. Someone called for an ambulance, and Marilyn carried on nibbling the nuts. Cuthburtson held on to his. Matron mopped up the mess with a rectangle of orange wool.

The Key

The old man on the bridge toll sat in a little wooden hut with gobs of mucus in the corner of his eyes, making him look sad, which he was mostly. He disliked 'College Boys' from Downleaze (stylish louts with good breeding and bad manners) only slightly less than he liked suicidal people. He resented *them* because he had given up a lucrative taxi business, owing to a heart condition, for a low-stress job. The suicide cases ambled along stark-faced or serene and never had the right change. Their eyes flickered briefly over the wooden sign with the Samaritans' phone number on it and they went and stared for ages at the three hundred foot column of space between the bridge and the scummy mudflats beneath. Then they would go away, leaving you relieved, and come back the following day, all smiles, and jump off. About once a year the suicidal people *were* boys from Downleaze College, and then the man at the toll bridge disliked them a little less, because he felt they were having a hard time there. Either that or all that good breeding made them a bit squiffy, like pedigree dogs. Any road, he felt a bit sorry for them, what with being so young and that. And he felt a bit sorry for the boys who came running past with bricks on their backs as a punishment. The thing about both the suicide boys and the brick boys was that they stood for reacting *against* the place. That's why he disliked them less than the other college boys, and why he was going to give Kieron three pass tickets even though he'd only just arrived. He knew the name of the game and he liked Kieron and his sort for not wanting to play it.

As he rounded the corner before Pearce House, Kieron put the bricks on his back and broke into a jog. When he saw the ambulance he came to a confused standstill. Mrs Cuthburtson and two ambulance staff were concealing the back entrance to the vehicle. A woman in a red suit was shouting, 'I'll take over, Caroline, don't worry!' and a plume of bright-coloured parents

171

stood on the steps, whilst others peered from the tall bay windows, glasses in hand.

'Hello, it's Tarzan!' shouted a voice from the front garden. Willy was standing with his parents holding a wine glass. 'Jesus, you didn't waste much time there, kiddo.'

'William,' said his mother, as if she weren't used to him by now.

'So you're the lad on the roof,' winked his father. 'Will's told us all about you,' and he stretched out a hand.

Kieron looked bewildered. 'What's happened here? Whose been hurt?'

'Cuthburtson's had his bollocks crushed,' said Willy, enjoying the effect on his mother. 'Elvis did it.'

'*Elvis?* Where is he now?'

'Probably been carted off to a loony bin.'

Kieron ran into the house by the back entrance, and up the stairs to the dormitories. Elvis's room was empty, so he went to his own room. There on the bed were the remains of his tracksuit and shirt, retrieved from the kiln by the caretaker, neatly folded. A note from Matron read: 'K – Do you want to keep these or shall I throw them away? Keep the name-tags. Matron.'

Picking them up he heard something jingle, and in the pocket he found a small keyring. He had put it there when they gave up trying to escape. On it was Eve's master-key.

He looked at his watch: it was one o'clock. He had one hour before he was due to see the head man. He ran out the back and down towards a small shop near the bridge to have a new key cut.

You could go your whole life without seeing a wedding, and then you went to two in one week, as if you could never know anyone who died and then loads of people you knew, or knew of, seemed to drop off like flies. It was like that with ambulances today. Kieron hadn't seen an ambulance at close range for years. Now they were appearing everywhere he turned. Coming out of the key shop, he saw an ambulance by the bridge, blue lights flashing.

Kieron ran up. A couple of men with yellow fluorescent jackets were speaking into walkie-talkies. There were no bodies in the back and no sign of blood or anything. He went over to the bridge-toll man.

'What's happened?'

'One of your lot just went over,' he said.

Kieron began to breathe very heavily, and ran to the edge of the bridge. He gripped the railings and strained as far as he could. A stretcher was being taken up the cliff path, but the person on it was covered with a sort of black plastic bin-liner. He felt his shirt bristle with sudden sweat. He ran back to the toll gate.

'Was it Elvis? You know – the little one – Elvis, was it him?'

'It wunt no bloody singer,' said the toll-gate man, shaking his head. 'All I know is 'twas one of your lot. I only saw him out the corner of my eye.'

He shook his head again with a bound-to-happen-sooner-or-later look which Kieron resented. Mostly because he thought that, with Elvis, it was. And he should have seen it. Poor Elvis, he'd told him to sod off last week. And Cuthburtson was giving him a hard time, and picking on him, and giving him humiliating punishments. No wonder he'd tried to crush his nuts. And of course, he'd have been sent out here to run ... Maybe Elvis had been trying to tell him something about Cuthburtson. Christ! It didn't bear thinking about. And no mother to ring him ever. Jesus, he'd been so unthinking. If only he could have hugged Elvis, *just once*. Just once. He saw himself running up to Elvis, grabbing hold of him in front of everyone, parents, teachers, Willy, everyone, and holding him so tight. He could almost feel how difficult it would be to get a purchase of the flimsy rib-cage, he could feel his bird-body trembling in his arms as he burst into sobs: 'Elvis! Elvis! I love you so much!' And he wouldn't care what they said, any of them, he would hug him to bits and rock him in his arms and they could all go to fuck.

The stretcher had reached the top of the cliff path and Kieron rushed up to meet it.

'Keep back!' said a policemen. 'There's nothing to see, son.'

'But it's my friend. I think it's my friend.'

The policeman's arm was a solid barrier in front of his chest. He was stung by the use of 'son' from a man two or three years older than himself. Through the drum-beats in his head he recalled his longing for drama: here it was, death on a cliff and a black bin-liner. He could see Elvis's elbow sticking out from the black plastic. He uncoiled and sprang forward.

'Let me come with him, *please!*'

He was jerked around in a savage pirouette ending against the cliff wall.

'It's all over. There's nothing for you to see, son.'

He watched the ambulance glide away and noticed that its blue light wasn't flashing. He walked to the centre of the bridge and looked out across the valley. The bridge-toll man started to sweat and took two Nurofen. He eyed Kieron with dismay. Just let that poor bugger jump off too and he was handing in his notice. These things never happened in ones. They always did it in droves, and it wasn't the end of the peak season yet.

Kieron stood staring out at the sheer cliffs for seven minutes. Then he shifted his weight and heard a clanking noise at his feet. Bending down, he saw the bright colours of a familiar object. He picked it up and turned it round in his hands. It was cold and wet. Bits of grit stuck to its shiny surface. He smoothed the squat buttocks and the sailor smirked at him. It was Joe's bottle.

'Oi! You, lad!' The bridge-toll man beckoned him over. 'There's no need to worry. They just told me – it can't have been your friend. I just saw this red and blue striped top, see, like you lot wear. But don't go worrying. It wasn't him.'

'I know.'

'Well, cheer up then,' said the toll-bridge man cheerlessly. 'It was only an old tramp.'

Dissidents

By four o'clock the headmaster had expelled Kieron, confiscated an obscene bottle from him and dismissed Miss Swanbrook.

Eve had tried to protest on Kieron's behalf. Even if the headmaster could cobble together some reasons for dismissing her, Kieron had done nothing. But the headmaster had looked at her with such defiance that she knew she was about to witness a moment of glory. He had placed his scoop on the desk in front of her, written in her own handwriting:

Dear Eve (is it OK if I call you that now?)
You were wonderful last night. I don't think I'm too young, really I don't, but I won't tell anyone at school.
Your lover,
XXX
PS. Do you really think it's illegal?

'And my source tells me you received two boys once at four o'clock in the morning.'

Eve gaped at it. She could already see the headlines of her curious and gruesome murder of her neighbour, Miss Crook, by letter bomb – cunningly not even addressed to her.

'But it's my writing,' she said in disbelief, slowly recalling how she had hoped to shock her neighbour 'How can it mean anything?'

He looked only momentarily uneasy. He knew this woman always had an answer to everything. But this time he had her fair and square.

'It's proof enough for me,' he said smugly.

It was his school. Everyone would back him.

Eve collected her things from the Art room and walked home carrying fruit and bones. As she entered her flat the phone was ringing. It was Cheryl (bilingual secretary, self-taught Jungian theorist and unpublished author of *Women Who Try Too Hard*). Eve explained that she had just been sacked and that she wouldn't make very good conversation.

'Have you ever asked yourself why you keep being attracted to the wrong sort of men?'

'Never.'

'Really?'

'Frequently.'

'And?'

'I've no idea.'

'Eve, the answer's staring you in the face.'

'You're going to tell me, "low self-esteem" or something.'

'No.'

'That's what you told me last month.'

'That stuff's old hat. Anyway, I've been thinking about you a lot. You find sex naughty, don't you?'

'Would it be any fun if you didn't?'

'You see? You associate sex with naughtiness, ie, *bad men*. You find yourself powerlessly attracted to wicked men, and the good, caring men you find some reason to reject.'

'Well, I would hardly associate Adrian with...'

'Intellectually, you know you want a kind man. But when it comes to the crunch, you just can't be turned on by them, can you?'

'It may have been...'

'So how does your self-conscious resolve this paradox? It's tried all the wicked men it can find and feels unhappy; it's tried all the good men and shies away. What does it do? It's clever, the subconscious, you know. It finds a kind, loving partner in a *wicked situation* ie, a pupil! See?'

'Well...' Eve was flicking through the corner of a coloured notepad and watching the television. She had turned the sound down when Cheryl rang, and could see Ian McCaskill caressing a warm front.

'It really is important to get your relationships sorted out. I know it might sound corny, Eve, but I care about you. If your friends can't help you, who can? I've been thinking about it for ages – you know I'm writing this self-help book – and it just sort of came to me the other day. In a flash. And now you've told me about this boy it all just falls into place. It's amazing. I'm glad I rang you. Now for goodness' sake, find a good man with no problems, Evie, before it's too late, or you'll end up with screwed-up relationships for life.'

'Thanks, Cheryl. Anyway, enough of me. How are you keeping? Are you still going out with that married Iranian fundamentalist?'

'He's *not* a fundamentalist, and he's Iraqi.'

'Sorry. That married Iraqi, then?'

'He's going to leave his wife. They haven't had sex for years.'

'Of course.'

'He *is*.'

'And convert to divorce, agnosticism and feminism?'

Cheryl thought Eve was being defensive.

As she put down the phone, Eve heard the letterbox clatter and the local paper plopped through the door. She scanned it to see the headlines of the scandal. But eclipsing the story was another headline: 'ANTI-CHRIST VICAR AT DOWNLEAZE COLLEGE'

The accompanying article described how the Reverend Arthur Hope had denounced religion. He had been caught daubing the words CO-OP STAMPS on the roof of the Christian Science building in large letters after JESUS SAVES. He had also written along the guttering: CHAOS AND CREATION. There was a picture of him, newly descended from the ladder, paintpot in hand, looking defiant and perky. His long strand of white hair, caught by the wind, was standing up like a Mohican's. In the caption he was quoted as saying: 'Chaos and creation: the world needs dissidents.'

Going to the Top

Eve lay on her bed, trying to reason out why she felt so indignant. She had behaved unprofessionally, there was no doubt about it. She had let herself be kissed. But somehow this was not the crime for which she was being punished. There was something else which made this punishment without evidence – this feverish search for evidence – seem so unfair. She rang Arthur Hope, but he was resting after a tiring morning at the police station.

'She had dark hair,' he said.

'Who did?'

'The woman Deanna reminded me of. I should have ... I let her go...'

'When?'

'Sixty years ago ... What waste!'

'Who was she?'

'She loved me.'

He sounded worn out. He was distraught at her news, and said he would ring the chairman of the governors himself, straight after his nap.

Eve thought about the situation. Cuthburtson was almost certainly guilty of child abuse, Felix had sexually assaulted her, Avery was grabbing anything in a school skirt and she, Eve, was being dismissed. Arthur was very tired. She decided to ring the chairman of the governors herself, and searched for his number in the school handbook.

'Hello,' said a woman.

'Hello,' said Eve. 'Could I speak to Mr Craven, please?'

'I'll just go and fetch him.'

'Hello,' came the voice, rather sternly, she thought.

She tried hard to think what she might say, but her impatience elbowed out all coherent thought.

'Hello, who's speaking?'

She waited numbly for her thoughts to get into single file. She crouched on the carpet, her nose inches from a stray yoghurt lid. A sinister quiver fizzed over her skin. He had spoken to her before.

The headmaster refused to see her. Daphne said he was fully booked well into the holidays. So she lay in wait for him and, as soon as he left his study, she followed him into the road.

'I didn't want to meet you so publicly,' she said, 'but I have some information which would be to your advantage.'

'I see,' said Mr Montague, uneasily heading towards his car. 'But I'm afraid it will have to wait. I'm in rather a hurry.'

'If you won't hear me in private, then I'll tell you here.'

The headmaster was walking very quickly now, eyes down to the pavement.

'Felix Lamb sexually assaulted me, Mr Cuthburtson is abusing a third-former, Mr Avery is having it off with half the sixth form, and the chairman of the governors is a pervert.'

At this he visibly flinched.

'How dare you ...!'

'The newspapers would have a field day with that, wouldn't they?'

'Are you threatening me with this nonsense, Miss Swanbrook?'

He stood by his car door and looked up. 'These are very serious allegations.' Then he sharpened his nose between the fingers of his spare hand and said resolutely: 'I don't think anyone would believe you.'

Eve pulled a cassette from her handbag. 'I just want you to listen to a copy of a recording I've made. They're obscene phone-calls. You might like to listen to them and reconsider a few things.'

She walked back to her car and drove off. Mr Montague wished he had followed his mother's advice and trained with the Prudential instead.

Running Away

Term ended on that Saturday. Today was Sunday, and the last remaining boarders would be cramming trunks and computers into the back of parents' cars. Eve had packed a large suitcase and all her painting things into her car and felt relieved to be leaving, though Elvis's tearful face after the end of final assembly kept nagging at her. In less than twelve hours she would be out of the country, and tomorrow she would be free to take a long view of things in the Tuscan sun.

She was nearing the toll gate on the bridge when she saw Kieron. He was lying in the road in front of her. She pulled to a halt near the car toll pay-machine and got out hurriedly.

'Kieron! What's happened?'

Kieron lay immobile and slowly turned his face towards her.

'I'm making a protest,' he said. 'You're not leaving unless you run over my body first.'

She breathed out with relief, and then she saw Elvis. He had tied himself to the car-toll barrier.

'And me,' he said, smiling. 'You'll have to kill me first too.'

Eve grinned. 'You'll have to get out of the way soon, there'll be other cars coming along.'

'We're not letting you go!' Elvis was radiant. 'You'll have to stay.'

Kieron was sitting up now and smiling at Eve. A car horn behind sent her running to her car.

'We'll talk in a sec. Hang on, I'll just shift this car.'

She put twenty pence in the slot and gripped the wheel in panic. Before her Elvis was propelled into the air at an angle of forty-five degrees like a human rocket.

'Let me down!' he cried meekly, clinging to the end of the barrier but still perpendicular to it.

'Quick! Drive through!' said Kieron. 'But wait on the other side.'

Promising

Behind her the barrier came down and Elvis could be released. She parked the car on the other side of the bridge and waited for them. The knots had tightened on Elvis under the strain. She looked in her rear-view mirror and saw Kieron apologising to the car behind. Then she saw him put his arms around Elvis and hold him tight. She turned around and watched them. His capacity to love. Then they ran up and Kieron got in the passenger seat.

'Right!' he said. 'Where are we going?'

'We're not going anywhere.'

'We're not letting you go,' said Elvis. 'If you go, I go.'

'I thought you were going anyway,' said Eve.

'I'm changing house,' said Elvis. 'They're putting me in Dawson House. I don't know what's happening to Cuthburtson. But I don't want to stay unless you're here.'

Eve looked at Elvis's upturned face as he crouched by the car door next to Kieron.

'Kieron will be here,' she said.

Elvis looked at the dashboard and stroked a furry sheep that was stuck onto it.

'I know. I'm glad he's not going. But please don't go. Please don't!'

'She's got to leave the school,' said Kieron. 'She's been dismissed.'

Elvis thumped his fists on the car door. 'It's not fair! It's not bloody fair!'

Eve looked at Kieron. 'Actually, I haven't been dismissed. Well, I was – like you – but I've been offered my job back. It's just that I don't want it.'

Elvis frowned and Kieron raised his eyebrows.

'But you've got to take it. If you don't, it'll be an admission of guilt,' Kieron said.

'But I am guilty.'

'You're not. And certainly not of what they're really accusing you of.'

'And what's that?'

'Not fitting their mould.'

Eve leant on the steering wheel and gazed at the grass verge and the road ahead.

'Don't you see?' he said. 'You're just running away.'

She was silent. Fifteen seconds passed. Then she turned to Elvis and said:

'Elvis, I'll do it for you. If you stay, I'll stay.'

Elvis shot to his feet and gave a whoop. Kieron laughed, got out of the car and hugged him.

'Now sod off,' he said, 'and let me talk to her alone.'

The Bridge

He got back in the car.

'I'm coming to Italy with you,' he said.

'That's not possible.'

'You mean you don't want me to.'

He could see she was going to be difficult. She had already conceded something to him and she wasn't letting him any closer.

'I've got all my stuff,' he said, indicating a pile of stuffed shopping bags which he began to throw from the verge into the back seat.

No reply.

'I'll drive you, if you like, when you get tired.'

No response.

'I'll protect you from all those men. You shouldn't travel alone, you know.'

She smiled at the steering wheel, but said nothing.

'I'll buy you a pizza.'

She got out of the car, walked on to the bridge and looked out at the view. He followed her, feeling that this was somehow a good sign. She would say something soon.

A vast valley lay before them. The sun must have been setting somewhere and left a cinematic glow on everything. The rock faces became denser in the evening shadows, and the depth of the valley, the height of the cliffs, were breathtaking.

'Did it mean anything to you?' he asked at last.

'Of *course* it did.'

She gripped the railings. He waited.

Still he waited.

'It must have been an amazing journey to get from one side of the valley to the other before they built the bridge,' she said.

That was pretty much in order, he thought. Change the subject.

'I bet,' he said, turning to look at her profile, 'that when they started to build the bridge, everyone said it was impossible. I bet everyone thought they were mad.'

She continued looking out at the cliffs.

'Two completely separate worlds,' she said, 'suddenly linked together so easily.'

Sod it. He pulled her elbow and forced her to look at him.

'But it *was* possible, wasn't it?'

'Yes,' she said.

She was looking at him, and he liked the way she was looking at him. He knew he was right, and he knew he had to show her the way.

'Take me to Italy with you!'

She stroked his hand.

'OK. In two years' time, I'll take you to Italy with me.'

They stood and looked at each other, and then he said:

'I've got a confession to make.' He looked at his watch. 'Right now there's a group of homeless people in your Art room – for the summer.'

'What?'

'I gave them a copy of your master key – you don't mind, do you?'

She smiled slowly. 'That's what I love about you!' and she squeezed him.

'What did you say? You love me? You did, you know.'

They stood looking at each other and smiling for quite a long time.

'Marry me!' he said suddenly.

Now this was really asking for trouble. It would be Don't be daft, Don't be ridiculous ... but what the hell?

'OK,' she said simply. 'Ask me in Italy. If you still want me then, then I will.'

'In two years' time?'

'Yes. But you won't.'

'I *will* ask you. No, I mean it. You don't believe me, do you? But I will.'

She kissed him slowly.

'I know.'

They walked to the car and she gave him his bags from the back. They had 'Sainsbury' on them in orange letters. He noticed it and shrugged. That was so long ago now.

He watched her drive away for the summer and was surprised

that he didn't feel sad. He stood on the bridge. He looked up at the optimism of its giant ironwork sprouting from the clifftops. You had to admire a bridge like that.

A selection of quality fiction from Headline

THE POSSESSION OF DELIA SUTHERLAND	Barbara Neil	£5.99 ☐
MANROOT	A N Steinberg	£5.99 ☐
DEADLY REFLECTION	Maureen O'Brien	£5.99 ☐
SHELTER	Monte Merrick	£4.99 ☐
VOODOO DREAMS	Jewell Parker Rhodes	£5.99 ☐
BY FIRELIGHT	Edith Pargeter	£5.99 ☐
SEASON OF INNOCENTS	Carolyn Haines	£5.99 ☐
OTHER WOMEN	Margaret Bacon	£5.99 ☐
THE JOURNEY IN	Joss Kingsnorth	£5.99 ☐
SWEET WATER	Christina Baker Kline	£5.99 ☐

All Headline books are available at your local bookshop or newsagent, or can be ordered direct from the publisher. Just tick the titles you want and fill in the form below. Prices and availability subject to change without notice.

Headline Book Publishing, Cash Sales Department, Bookpoint, 39 Milton Park, Abingdon, OXON, OX14 4TD, UK. If you have a credit card you may order by telephone – 01235 400400.

Please enclose a cheque or postal order made payable to Bookpoint Ltd to the value of the cover price and allow the following for postage and packing:

UK & BFPO: £1.00 for the first book, 50p for the second book and 30p for each additional book ordered up to a maximum charge of £3.00.

OVERSEAS & EIRE: £2.00 for the first book, £1.00 for the second book and 50p for each additional book.

Name ....

Address ....

....

....

If you would prefer to pay by credit card, please complete:
Please debit my Visa/Access/Diner's Card/American Express (delete as applicable) card no:

Signature .... Expiry Date ....